S0-DTB-532

THE QUADRA CHRONICLES

BRUCE BRADBURN
Illustrations by Rhys Haug

BOOK PUBLISHERS NETWORK

Book Publishers Network
P.O. Box 2256
Bothell • WA • 98041
Ph • 425-483-3040
www.bookpublishersnetwork.com

Copyright © 2013 by Bruce Bradburn

All rights reserved. No part of this book may be reproduced, stored in, or introduced into a retrieval system, or transmitted in any form, or by any means (electronic, mechanical, photocopying, recording, or otherwise) without the prior written permission of the publisher.

10 9 8 7 6 5 4 3 2 1

Printed in the United States of America

LCCN   2013942636
ISBN   978-1-937454-88-3

Editor: Julie Scandora
Cover design: Laura Zugzda
Interior design: Stephanie Martindale

Contents

Acknowledgments

I wish to thank my lovely wife for her encouragement and the occasional push to get this book into print. I also wish to thank all of those who have shared with me their experiences with river otters.

Book One

The Journey
Commences

Chapter one
Oscar Arrives

The spring morning was as lovely as any you could possibly imagine. The sun glinted off the crystalline water, and a soft breeze whispered through the boughs of the small evergreens, which guarded the mouth of a quaint bay on a much larger island.

In a cozy den on the north side of the small island, a mother river otter was giving birth to a trio of offspring. Their furry bodies cuddled close to their mother, although they could not yet open their eyes to see her.

As she lay admiring her beautiful brood, she began thinking of names for these newcomers to her world. The female, who was the first to arrive, had a gracious and charming look to her, and the mother otter thought that such a child would make a perfect Octavia.

Her two brothers were already all boys, poking at each other from the moment of their birth. The larger of the two, the second-born, she would call Omar, due to his sleek body and dark brown fur. The third, and by far the most active, was a little fellow who could be none other than an Oscar. She admired and loved them equally, of course, but she already knew that Oscar would always have a special place in her heart.

The baby otters, called kits, stayed in their nursery with their mother. The den was lined with leaves, grass, and hair and was warm and comforting. The mother stayed with them most of the time, leaving the den only to hunt for food for herself. Even though her babies would not open their eyes for about a month, she knew they were safe in the den, which had a very narrow entrance.

The boys amused themselves by roughhousing and, on occasion, getting in a jab at Octavia, who pretended not to notice. Their first month of life was, therefore, quite uneventful with their mother always at hand to provide food, warmth, and the frequent cuddle. The kits grew quickly and were delighted when they were first able to open their eyes and look out the doorway of their den and see the water and scenery outside.

They still stayed inside for several weeks, but every time Mother Otter came back to the den, she would find all three of them crowded at the doorway, each trying to get the best view. The sight of three little noses and six tiny eyes always made her smile to herself. She knew that soon she would be able to bring them outside to start the task of becoming independent. They had so much to learn, and she looked forward to becoming a teacher as well as a mother.

Chapter two
The Swimming Lesson

Within the next month, Mother Otter knew the time was right for the young ones to venture forth. The first task she had was to teach them to swim for without that skill they would not survive. Although she knew there were few natural predators, especially on this lovely island, there were stories of young otters being carried off by eagles. The best way of eluding these great birds was to swim fast and dive deep, and so she began her training with these most basic of abilities.

She took each kit down to the water's edge and gently placed it in the clear, cool salt water. She then showed how to paddle with its tiny webbed feet.

When each had mastered the basic paddling motion, she then demonstrated for them an intricate combination of flexing her hind legs and tail. The kits watched in amazement as she sped through the water and dove down out of their sight. She stayed underwater for what seemed like forever, and when she surfaced, she was many yards away. The kits could not wait to try this new move, but Mother made them each do it separately, under her watchful eye.

As Mother Otter had expected, Octavia was the most graceful and seemed to slip through the water effortlessly. Every aspect of her movement was like a symphony. Octavia made a graceful circle of their little cove and returned to the shore to the broad smile of her mother. Omar was next and also took readily to the new motion. He already displayed great strength, and Mother could see he would be a fast swimmer and deep diver.

Oscar had been waiting most impatiently as his siblings showed off their new skill, and he was beside himself when Mother finally told him to try. He leapt into the water and began to paddle furiously and flex every part of his body at once. Needless to say, he did not make much progress, but he did make Octavia and Omar double over in laughter while Mother just sighed and knew she had her work cut out for her.

Through the next few weeks, Mother Otter spent extra time with Oscar, and he eventually was able to grasp the concept of just flexing his hind legs and tail and not his entire body. He still did not have Octavia's style or Omar's strength, but Mother felt he had progressed enough to survive and was now ready to proceed to teach her young ones to hunt for food.

At first, she had them dive with her to identify their prey. The crabs, clams, mussels, and oysters were easy since only the crabs moved, and they were no match for the speed of the otters. The biggest problem for the youngsters was to break open the shell for their meal. Mother Otter was very adept at opening even the tough oysters and showed them all of her tricks for opening the shells. They soon were enjoying a great feast on the shore of their cove and were most proud of themselves for their hunting success.

However, Mother Otter now had to show them how to catch the mainstay of their diet: fish, not the fast-moving salmon but a wide variety of bottom fish, which were generally slow-moving or living in holes in the rocks. She would show the kits her technique for catching the fish and then bring them close to the young ones and release them so they could catch them on their own.

Oscar found this to be great fun and really had a grand time catching, releasing, re-catching, releasing, and catching again. Finally, his mother had to explain to him that the object was actually to eat the fish and not just catch them. She told him that when he was on his own he would have to hunt most of the day just to survive. She told all of her young that this was very important since their bodies burned up a lot of energy just to keep warm in the cool water.

Octavia and Omar grasped this right away, but Oscar was so full of energy and enthusiasm that he could not imagine that he had to work for his energy. Mother could only sigh again and hope that Oscar would learn this lesson before going off on his own and have to learn it under less sheltered conditions.

Chapter three
Discoveries – Good and Bad

Once securing food had been learned, Mother Otter could move on to other aspects of otter behavior that the young ones needed to learn to fit into the larger otter community. Even though otters tend to live alone, except for mothers and their young, a great part of their time is spent playing with others of their kind. This play is used to form bonds between the basically solitary animals and also allows for the exchange of hunting tips and the techniques for marking individual territories. It was not surprising that Oscar excelled in this new lesson. Although he enjoyed his play with his siblings, the prospect of meeting new friends provided a great incentive for him.

This new stage of training also provided the youngsters with the opportunity to explore the surrounding territory—under Mother's watchful eye, of course. They first ventured south around Heriot Island, where their den was, to look into Heriot Bay. Mother explained that, although it seemed peaceful enough, there was a large ferryboat that came into the bay six times a day. It was easily avoided with their speed, but Mother pointed out the piers around the ferry dock, which she knew would be an irresistible temptation as a place to play.

She explained that, when the ferry docked, great currents were created by its propellers and the small fry could be sucked into the blades or slammed into the pilings. Octavia and Omar took this in with serious expressions of concern, but Oscar thought it might be fun to be swept away by mighty currents and tossed about. Again, Mother could only sigh and hope for the best for her youngest.

There was also a marina in the bay and lots of activity around the docks in this beautiful late spring weather. The people on the boats loved to see the little otter family swimming around them, diving out of sight, and then popping up a ways away. Some of the boats had large dogs on them, and Oscar immediately found a great game to play. Whenever he saw a dog on the dock, he would swim under it and make noises so the dog would notice him. He would then scramble around while the dog set to frantic barking, disturbing all around. The owners would then have to come and take the dog back to their boat. Oscar thought this was grand fun.

There was a large protected bay next to Heriot Bay known as Drew Harbor. Many boats would moor here during the spring and summer, and the otters made friends with all of the children who would row about in dinghies. While this was much fun, the young otters noticed that sometimes the water smelled a bit unusual, not like the wonderful freshness of the water near the den.

Mother Otter explained that the boats sometimes discharged material into the harbor, which caused the funny smell. She also explained that the shellfish in the harbor could cause them to get sick if they ate it. Oscar, of course, had to find out for himself by nibbling on a clam he retrieved from the bottom of the harbor. That night, he had a terrible stomachache and had to stay in the den for the next two days until he felt well enough to join his brother and sister in their explorations. Mother was thankful that this little experiment of Oscar's was not more serious, and she hoped that it would teach him a lesson.

Chapter four
Horizons Expand

The exploration of Drew Harbor, however, was an ongoing adventure. The three baby otters found the water warm and a great place to play, with an enthusiastic audience of children to applaud their antics. Octavia and Omar were the stars of the show with their graceful swimming and diving, while Oscar provided the comic relief. Although the harbor was fun and close to home, Oscar felt some strange stirrings within him that urged him to expand his horizons. He pressed his mother to do further explorations, and she was most happy to oblige.

Leaving their den one morning, Mother Otter had her brood swim north along the rocky shore and venture into every tiny inlet along the way. They found excellent hunting grounds with lots of shellfish and small fish on which to dine. They finally came to a small bay with a channel at one end between the shore and a very small islet. The water was beautifully clear in the bay, and the channel was almost dry when they arrived.

Mother Otter told them it became completely dry at low tide and the bottom was covered with nets, under which were vast clam beds, which were tended by people who sometimes came in by boat to harvest. She warned them about trying to go under the nets in search of clams. She showed them how to dig at the edges and find all they could eat. There were also many oysters, and the family had a grand repast on a small beach on the islet.

Oscar noticed two large floats just off the shore of the main island and struck off to investigate. He discovered that one float had been constructed such that he could not get into the area between the decking and the flotation pontoons as he did at the marina. The other float did provide access to this space, and Oscar immediately thought this would be a perfect place to play his dog game—if he could only find a dog.

On the floats, the entire family found the ideal spot for a nap in the warm sun. While the kits lolled around with their full tummies, Mother gave them a short geography lesson. She told them they were now on the shore of Hyacinthe Bay, which was very quiet, especially compared to the hustle and bustle of Heriot Bay. There was, however, an abundance of wildlife in the area, although not always in evidence.

Mother pointed out the tall, ungainly looking great blue heron stalking small fish in the shallows near the islet. She also showed the kits the two kingfishers vying for the same dinner with the heron. They fished in a different manner, flying over the surface of the water until they spotted a fish. Then they would hover over it, gauging its speed, direction, and depth, and suddenly fold their wings back and dive into the water. The young otters were amazed that these birds were able to dive so well. They made Oscar wish that he could fly, but he was enjoying his relaxation too much to think very seriously about it.

Suddenly, a strange shadow crossed the float. Mother Otter screamed at her young and shoved them unceremoniously into the water and under the float. The three youngsters had never seen their mother in such a state and were both puzzled and worried. After a bit, Mother slipped out and popped her head above the surface. When she returned, she told them all to stay put for a while longer. All three started talking at once, asking their mother what was going on.

She explained that the strange shadow they had seen was that of a bald eagle who would have liked nothing more than to grab a fat, happy little otter for his dinner. This lesson of constant vigilance was one taken to heart by all three. Even Oscar could understand that not learning this could be a fatal mistake. This time Mother sighed with relief.

After several more minutes, Mother decided that they had had enough excitement for one day and led the way out from under the float. The tide had gone out by this time, so they swam to shore and scampered down the now-dry channel back to the little bay. They could see the entire channel was covered by the nets of the clam farmers.

Oscar marked this place in his mind; it looked like the perfect spot to get a free meal without all of the work of hunting. During the scamper down the channel, Mother Otter kept her eye out for any other signs of large circling birds. She did spot one and stopped the children to show them the turkey vulture lazily soaring overhead. She pointed out how to tell this bird from the eagle by its head and the configuration of the feathers on the wingtips.

As they entered the water again to swim to their den, they all looked up on the hillside above the bay. There was a large house with a huge deck overlooking the water. Mother Otter told them she had heard it was an inn where people came to relax but she had also seen quite a number of children there during the summer months. Oscar filed this away, too, since he knew that where there were children, there were usually dogs, and he had already found a good spot for his dog game on the one float.

What with the excitement of the eagle and finding a wonderful place to feast on shellfish, after the swim back to their den, the kits all curled up and slept for a very long time. They were really getting to know their part of the world.

Chapter five
Farther North

During the next few months through the summer, Mother Otter took her young even farther north exploring all of Hyacinthe Bay, around the corner into Open Bay, and out to the Breton Islands. On the way to Open Bay, they passed some rocks where the kits saw their first seals sunning themselves on the rocks and looking comical with their heads and tails sticking up at each end and their bellies resting on the rocks.

The kits watched in amusement as a seal clumsily worked its way into the water. However, the instant it went under, the otters were astounded at the speed and grace of the animal. Even though the seals were much larger than the otters, they were even quicker in the water, and they could dive much deeper and stay under longer.

The youngsters asked their mother why the seals could lie around all day and did not have to hunt all of the time like otters. Mother told them that unlike otters, seals had a layer of fat, called blubber, under their skin which was a natural insulator against the cold water. This meant that they did not have to eat all of the time to stay warm. She also told them that due to their size, seals did not have to worry about flying predators attacking them, so they could afford to lie about on land.

She explained that the seals' greatest threat was in the water from killer whales, or orcas, who liked seal meat just as much as they liked salmon. The orcas could swim even faster than the seals and dive even deeper and generally travelled in large groups, or pods, making them especially dangerous for the seals

Oscar began to picture himself as a seal: big and fast and graceful and not having to hunt all of the time. Then he thought of the eagle and pictured himself as some sort of combination of the two that would be able to escape the orcas by leaping from the water and taking flight.

When he shared this thought with Octavia and Omar, they looked at him in total confusion and then burst out laughing. Mother also joined in and told her young kit that he should be happy being what he was. When Oscar finally put together his own mental picture of a creature looking like the ungainly seal but with wings soaring through the air, even he had to laugh.

Just around the east end of Open Bay, there was a beautiful channel between the large land mass of Quadra Island and many small rocks. The family used this channel on their way up to explore Village Bay and, along the way, found an abundance of food and several other otters with whom they stopped and played as a break in their explorations. One of the otters they met showed them where he had found a smooth chute in the rocks that ran from high up a hill right down to the water. He scrambled up and then slid down the chute on his belly, making a large splash when he hit the water. The kits were quick to join in the fun and spent hours sliding down the hill into the water. Their mother even made a few runs and had as much fun as her young.

"He scrambled up and then slid down the chute on his belly..."

One day, after spending far too much time in the chute, Mother Otter realized that they were a long way from their den and probably could not make it back before dark. She decided that this would be the time for an overnight stay away from home. She led them even farther north until she came to an opening between a small island called Bold Island and Quadra. This led to a lovely crescent-shaped channel, which was completely protected.

As they swam through this channel, they came upon something that was the answer to Oscar's dream of finding free food. There, along the shore of Bold Island, were hundreds of marker floats, and under each one were strings of oysters or mussels, just waiting to be plucked off and eaten. All four of them had a wonderful time eating as much as they could hold of a variety of tasty shellfish.

They found a cozy little den that had been abandoned by some other animal and settled in for the night, enjoying another giant meal in the morning before returning to their own den. The only drawback to this find was the fact that it was so far away from home. However, Oscar determined that when he established his own den, it was going to be much closer to this glorious seafood buffet.

Chapter six
A Change of Season

One morning, Oscar noticed that the sun was not quite as warm as it had been and that many of the boats at the marina and in Drew Harbor had gone. The water was also cooler, and Mother explained that a new season had arrived: fall. The days were also getting shorter and the nights longer and colder, but this did not bother Oscar as much as the absence of children and dogs to play with. He made up for it by teasing Octavia and Omar until they had had too much, at which point, they would pounce and then sit on him until he calmed down. Mother would just leave the den and hunt so she did not have to referee.

The fall also brought the first storms the kits had seen. Their den was on the north side of Heriot Island, so they did not get the prevailing winds directly in their front door, but they could see the large waves and the rain pounding on the water and shore. It was snug and warm in their den, and when they went out to hunt, they were beneath the big waves and did not really notice the bad weather, but it was not as much fun as Oscar had remembered in the spring and summer.

In fact, it was a lot less fun since Mother Otter decided that because they did not spend as much time out exploring she would use the time for a little classroom training of her young. Oscar did not think much of this new school routine, and it was a constant challenge for his mother to keep his attention. Octavia and Omar were apt students as Mother explained such things as territory selection and marking, how to select a spot for a proper den, and the otter rules of etiquette regarding play and respecting each other's territories.

The time seemed to drag for Oscar as the storms grew more frequent and violent, and then one morning, the world changed. As the youngsters peeked out the doorway of their den, they could barely see but a few feet. All was white, but not like the foggy mornings of fall. This white was made up of many small dots falling from the sky. Oscar stuck his nose out, and one of the dots landed on the end. It was very cold and disappeared immediately on contact with his warm little nose. He jumped back inside the den, and Octavia and Omar were the next to experience the cold, disappearing white dots. Mother Otter laughed at her young and told them it was snow.

The snow lasted for several days but would ease up periodically, and the kits could see the shores of all of the islands covered with a fluffy white blanket. They ventured out from time to time and discovered that the snow was a great deal of fun to play in. They made up several games, which usually ended up with Octavia and Omar pushing Oscar into a large pile of snow. It was so much fun that he did not mind at all.

Finally, the snow stopped, and the sun came out to reveal a spectacular scene. The clear skies lasted for several days, and the temperature dropped dramatically. One morning, Mother Otter gathered her brood and took them off to Drew Harbor. The mouth of the harbor was open, but at the south end, where the water was quite shallow, there was a strange, hard coating on the water. Mother told them this was ice and it was one of the best things to play on. She scrambled up on the hard, cold surface, took off at a brisk pace and then picked up her feet and slid along on her belly. The kits remembered sliding down the rock chute by Village Bay and how much fun that had been, so they immediately followed their mother's lead.

They found they could slide on the ice for very long distances and end up either tumbling into a snow bank on the shore or actually going off the ice and into the water with a big splash. These games continued for hours. Some people came out on the shore of the harbor to watch the four of them playing and laughed and clapped at each spectacular slide.

Oscar was not the only one who enjoyed performing for the audience, and the kits took turns trying to outdo each other in how far or fast they could slide. Octavia and Omar definitely had the advantage when it came to the speed and distance, but neither could match Oscar for the fantastic finishes to his slides. When he went into a snow bank, all that could be seen were legs and a tail going in all directions and finally a little furry head popping up out of the snow. Mother Otter let them play until it was almost dark and then herded them back to the den, stopping on the way to eat. They all slept until very late the next morning but could not wait to get back to the ice.

The ice lasted for nearly a week, which Mother Otter said was quite unusual for the harbor. When the ice finally melted, the kits were disappointed but filed away some great memories with hopes for more cold weather. For Oscar, this had been a perfect break from school, but now their mother ushered them back into the classroom. They were now well into winter, and one day, Mother told them they might have a visitor soon. They were a little puzzled by this, but their mother would not tell them any more.

"When he went into a snow bank ..."

Chapter seven
The Visitor

One morning, they were all awakened by a rustling and scratching outside the entrance to their den. They opened their eyes to see another pair of eyes staring at them from the doorway. The eyes were followed by the body of another otter coming into their den. The kits were very much alarmed and squeaked in terror and hid behind their mother.

Mother did not seem upset at all and turned to them and introduced their father. The three youngsters did not know what to say. They had never even heard their mother mention their father in all of their training. Oscar was the first to recover his composure and venture out from behind his mother to greet the stranger. The two of them hit it off immediately.

After gathering some shellfish and catching a few fish for breakfast, the little family retreated into the den to get to know one another. Oscar was bursting with questions for his father, who was more than willing to oblige his youngster with answers. It turned out that Father was quite the world traveler who had a very large territory of his own and had journeyed to many places outside. It took him almost a year to make the rounds of his own territory, but sometimes that stretched out even longer if he got off on a side trip.

All of the kits loved the stories of their father's wanderings as he told them of having gone completely around the large island of Quadra and beyond to islands and inlets they had not even heard of. He spoke of dangerous places, such as Surge Narrows, Hole in the Wall, and the Yuculta Rapids, in which he had seen even very large boats thrown about like sticks. He also told of calm and intriguing channels between islands, like Whiterock Passage, of beautiful and serene coves and bays, and of places like the Octopus Group teeming with all sorts of fish and shellfish.

Oscar was mesmerized by these tales and pressed his father for details of how he was able to cover such vast distances. Oscar knew he would never be able to swim to those places, even in a year. Father explained that there were many tricks to his travels, including learning how to ride the currents without having to expend energy swimming, and how to hitch a ride on a passing chunk of driftwood. These were fine if the currents and driftwood were going in the direction you wanted to go, his father said, but if you wanted to go some other direction, you needed to use the devices of men. The safest he said were the large booms of logs being towed by tugboats because the men on the tugboats never came back onto the booms, and there were plenty of places to hide in them if predators like eagles happened to be about.

The method that fascinated Oscar the most was hitching a ride on one of the swift cruisers like he had seen in the marina. His father explained that this was risky since a lot of the boats had a dog on board and most of their traveling was done during daylight hours, so it was easy to be seen.

He said he always watched for boats with low swim platforms at the stern that had a dinghy or other items tied on. He would use these as hiding places while the boat was under way and then slip quietly off before the boat came into a dock or started to drop its anchor. He had used this technique many times to get to some really faraway places. Father regaled the kits with tales for several hours until Mother said it was time for them to get some sleep. They all complained a bit but were promised more stories in the morning. Oscar went to sleep with many visions dancing about in his head and dreamed of seeing these sights on his own.

Father stayed around for almost a month, and the family played and hunted during the day and early evening but would then snug down in their den to listen to more tales of travels. They heard of the time that Father had almost gone all the way to Alaska because he got too comfortable in a little den he had made for himself on a log boom. The weather was very bad so he had not wanted to go out. He found plenty of food among the logs and did not peek outside for several days. When he finally did, he did not recognize anything around him and realized he was now much farther north than he had ever been.

Luckily, the weather got so bad that the tug and log boom had to pull into a sheltered cove, which was shared by a number of boats also sitting out the storm. He swam around the boats and heard that one of them was going to head back south as soon as the weather lifted. Checking out this boat, he was able to discover a wonderful hiding place that even had a place for him to store some food for the trip. He spent the next few days gathering shellfish and storing them away. He also found the galley on the boat unattended one day and discovered a bowl of eggs out on the counter. He was able to make off with half a dozen before he heard someone coming and scuttled off to his lair. The cook made quite a fuss over the missing eggs and told the crew that there would be no custard for dessert that night.

Their father also told the kits of many large and dangerous animals he had seen on his journeys but assured them they did not have to worry about them where they were around Quadra. Naturally, this made Oscar want to go exploring even more. He could think of nothing more exciting than travel but hoped he could do it with a minimum of effort. Both Mother and Father tried to convince Oscar that he had lots to learn before setting off to see the world but doubted they had gotten through to the young one.

One day when winter was finally on its way out and spring was just around the corner, they could see across the channel a tugboat with a large barge in tow moving north. The barge was loaded with a lot of equipment and some trailers and even a small cruiser. Father said it was probably the makings of a logging camp that would be set up when spring arrived and he should probably be on his way to check it out. The family said a tearful goodbye, and Father struck out to catch up with the tugboat and barge. He left them with a promise that he would return next winter with more tales.

Chapter eight
More Changes

Mother Otter assured the kits that they would see their father again but told them it was time to get back to their lessons since they were coming up on a full year of age and it would soon be time for them to go off and set up their own dens and territories. The young ones were a bit surprised by this, but they knew this was what all of the training was for. Mother Otter told them that she loved them all but there would be a new litter coming along soon and they needed to make room for their new brothers and sisters.

Mother knew that Octavia and Omar were almost ready to be off on their own, but she did have a few worries about Oscar. Octavia had already scouted out an area for her den in the Breton Islands, and Omar had found a perfect spot for himself around the corner of Read Island. Mother felt that she should try to encourage Oscar to stay a little closer so she could keep an eye on him during the first month or two of his independence. She dropped a few sly hints about the easy pickings for food around the little islet on Hyacinthe Bay. Oscar remembered the great feasting on the clams and oysters and the warm water of the shallow channel, but what really sealed the deal for him were the float where he could play the dog game and the prospects of having children around for an audience for his antics. He told his mother that he was going to explore the area right away for a possible den site, and she once more heaved a great sigh of relief.

Oscar spent the next few weeks swimming all around the islet and the bays and coves. His first thought was the islet itself and so decided to explore it. When he came ashore off the channel with the clam nets, he sensed he was being watched. He also detected a distinct scent, as if the area had already been marked. However, it did not smell like an otter, and he had not encountered one there before, so he decided to examine it further.

He scrambled up the rocks of the small beach where they had had their great feast and checked out the two parts of the islet. The section to the south was a rather tall hill and looked like far too much effort to scale, so he opted for the area to the north. As he came around the corner of a rock, he came face to face with four small black eyes peering out of a crack. He jumped back, startled, but then stopped and introduced himself. Two minks inched out of the crack and warily eyed the stranger but did not say anything. Oscar went on to explain that he was looking for a den and had just happened upon this spot. The two minks stayed where they were but informed Oscar this was their den, and they were there first.

Oscar looked around and decided there was an abundance of most suitable territory for a den and apologized to the minks for disturbing them. He said that he liked the area and planned to find himself another place nearby but that he would not try to take away their home. This seemed to please the minks who then came out of their den and introduced themselves to Oscar. They said they had lived there for over five years and had been very happy. They told him there was plenty of food and no one came around to bother them. The people who worked the clam beds just came every so often, and there was a dog that sometimes came with them. They also said there was a dog that sometimes lived at the big house by the small bay but he had never really been a threat. Oscar became very excited by this news: TWO DOGS! What fun he could have on the float!

To celebrate, Oscar invited the minks down to the beach for lunch. Sensing a good friendship, they agreed, and soon, all three were busily gathering clams and oysters. One of the minks went out into the water by the float and caught several rock crabs to add, and they had a marvelous time. After eating, Oscar said goodbye to the minks and went off in search of another site for his home. He had not gone far along the south shore of Hyacinthe Bay when he noticed a tiny cove.

Swimming into it, he could see what appeared to be an opening in the rocks. Upon examination, he found an abandoned den of some other creature. There was practically no scent remaining in the area, so Oscar knew it had been vacated a number of years ago. It would need a little clean up, but it would provide great shelter from the wind and waves, and there were plenty of leaves and moss around to make it comfortable. He was VERY excited and could not wait to get back and tell the rest of his family about his find and his new friends.

That night, the three youngsters all told their mother about where they planned to set up housekeeping when the time came for them to leave. Mother Otter was very pleased and offered each of them a few tips on how to equip and care for their homes. For once, even Oscar seemed to be paying attention, and Mother Otter knew the time was near for the kits to be on their own.

Chapter nine
Off on His Own

So it was that two weeks later Mother Otter gathered her young around her, gave each a big hug and kiss, and sent them on their ways. She was happy to see the enthusiasm in their eyes, sad to see them go, and excited in looking forward to her new litter. She also knew they were not going so far away that she would not see them often, which also gave her a good feeling. Her only misgivings had to do with her youngest and what sort of mischief he would get into, but she put those thoughts out of her mind and set about getting the den ready for the next inhabitants.

With tremendous excitement and enthusiasm and only a few worries, Oscar paddled off on his own and into his new world of adventure.

HARDLY THE END

BOOK TWO

Settling In

Chapter one
New Homes

After spending their first year of life with their mother learning the skills they would need to survive on their own, the three young otters each set up their new dens. Omar, although not the oldest but the largest and strongest of the three, had found a wonderful little inlet on the eastern shore of Read Island, on the Sutil Channel. His was the most remote of the new dens from that of their mother, but Omar enjoyed the solitude, and his home provided fantastic views of the channel with its boating activity and Cortes Island across from his den. He could also see all the way to the mountains on the mainland far in the distance. With plenty of good hunting and no other otters nearby, he had the place pretty much to himself, but he was close enough to his mother and siblings that he could drop in for a visit from time to time, as the mood suited him.

Octavia had found what to her was the absolutely perfect place to live: a cozy little den in the small group of islands known as the Bretons, right where the Hoskyn Channel split off from the larger Sutil Channel. There were hundreds of seals who sunned themselves at low tide on the rocks off these islands, and she enjoyed watching their antics. During the spring and on into the fall, many kayakers came by to watch the seals as well, and they would stop on the Bretons for picnics. They proved to be a great source of amusement when Oscar showed her how to raid their lunches. She was also quite close to the rock chute she and her family had used as a water slide, which provided much fun.

Oscar had stayed closest to Mother's den, which she had subtly arranged so she could keep an eye on her youngest, but his den on the south shore of Hyacinthe Bay was just perfect for him. He had clams and oysters right at his door, and he had made friends with the two minks who lived on the tiny islet just around the corner. The three of them would get together at least once a week to have lunch on one of the beaches on their islet. Oscar had really settled in.

One morning, while he was still sleepy after having had a huge late-night feast on shellfish, Oscar was awakened by a rustling outside of the door to his den. Not knowing what might be outside, he decided to make a quick getaway. Gathering his feet under him, Oscar launched himself through the opening to his den and directly into the water, with a lot of noise and a big splash. When he surfaced, he spun around in the water to see what had been the source of the noise outside his den. All he caught was a glimpse of a flicking tail disappearing into the woods.

He had to laugh at himself. He had been frightened by one of the most gentle creatures around—a young deer. With his loud explosion from the den, he had certainly frightened the deer even more than he had been. Oscar hoped that the deer would come back so he could make friends with it since he was always looking for someone to play with.

Since he was now up, Oscar decided to go for a little swim around the bay to see if anyone else was up. As he came into the shallow area at the north end of the bay, he spotted a family of raccoons marching along, single-file, at the edge of the water. He swam in close to shore and was prepared to get out on the beach to introduce himself when the mother raccoon suddenly turned toward him, arched her back, and hissed loudly. Oscar was very startled at this rather unfriendly attitude and slipped back into the water. As he swam on his way, he remembered how protective his mother had been of her brood and decided that he would wait to make friends with the young ones until they were a little older and out from under the protection of their mother.

As he completed his circuit of the bay, he could see the tide had gone very far out, and the people who tended the clam beds under the nets in the channel between the minks' islet and the big island had come in by boat to harvest. They had brought their dog with them, and Oscar hurried back to the end of the channel where the floats were to see if he could get the dog out onto the floats so he could play his dog game. Oscar loved to get up under the decking of a float and make noises to attract dogs, which would then scramble around on the decking, setting up a tremendous barking, and have to be disciplined by their owners.

He could clearly see the clammers' dog on the shore and went out to the float and made quite a bit of noise to attract his attention. However, much to his disappointment, the dog stayed with his masters and would not venture out to the float. Oscar had never experienced such rejection and had no idea what he could do to lure the dog into getting into trouble. After giving it some thought, he had only succeeded in getting a headache, so he went back to his den to take a nap, but he knew the challenge had to be met.

Chapter two
New Arrivals

As spring moved into summer, Oscar found great pleasure in his new home. He had finally been able to make contact with the fawn he had startled so badly, and they became fast friends. Although the deer could not swim under water and did not eat fish or shellfish, he would come over to the little islet and have lunch with Oscar and the two minks on a regular basis. The four of them made quite a sight on the beach munching away on their foods of choice and playing in the warm sunshine.

The deer finally got Oscar to climb up to the high part at the south end of the islet, and from there, Oscar could see all the way to Octavia's den in the Bretons. He could also spy just the very southern tip of Read Island and knew Omar's home was right around the corner. He could also see down to his mother's den where the new litter was undergoing the same training that Oscar and his siblings had gone through. The view was spectacular, and he vowed not to avoid scaling the height as he had on his first visit. The four friends made the climb a regular feature of their luncheon meetings.

One early summer morning when Oscar had decided to sleep in, he was awakened by the joyous sound of children's laughter and realized it was quite close by. Slipping quietly into the water, he swam slowly around the tip of land toward the floats and the islet. On one of the floats, he saw four young children, three girls and one boy, playing and looking into the clear water. Oscar took a deep breath and swam under water to the place the children were peering down. He then popped his head out of the water just a few feet from where they were. They all jumped back and squealed in startled excitement but recovered quickly at the sight of Oscar's furry little face, long whiskers, and dark eyes.

Oscar spent quite a bit of time entertaining the children with his underwater antics. He had great fun showing off his tricks and his fishing skill. The children loved to watch him dive down, catch a fish, and then pop to the surface with the fish in his mouth, head and tail sticking out both sides. They clapped their hands and laughed approval at each new catch. Oscar was having so much fun that he completely forgot himself and ate far too much. He finally just lay on his back on the surface with his bulging little tummy sticking out of the water.

Finally, just as Oscar was about to swim back to his den for a bit of a nap, the parents of the children came down to the float. Oscar realized there were two families and remembered his mother had told him that in the summer a number of children came to stay in the big house above the bay at one end of the channel. He had hoped they would bring a dog with them that he could tease on the floats, but these folks did not appear to have one. They did, however, provide something else for him to do.

The parents slipped life jackets on the children and got out a couple of kayaks to give rides to their children. Oscar could swim alongside the kayaks and then dive down under them as they paddled around the islet and the bay. All in all, it was a grand time, and Oscar could tell that it was going to be lots of fun to have these people around to entertain. He did decide, though, that he would remember to eat less the next time he wanted to show off his hunting skill. He left the families on their kayaks and swam slowly back to his den for a well-deserved nap

Chapter three
Finally!

T he children and their families stayed for over a week, and Oscar had a marvelous time performing for them. One day, Oscar and his friends, the minks and the fawn, were having their usual lunch meeting when all four of the children came down to the floats. The tide was not all the way out so there was still water in the channel that was too deep for the children to wade across to the islet. However, they had quite a treat to see this group together. When the three had finished lunch, the fawn waded back across the channel and walked very near to the children. They were truly awed to see the deer this close and stayed very still so as not to frighten it. When the fawn had left, the little boy ran up to the big house to tell the parents about their special experience.

The parents came down to the float to see Oscar and the minks on the beach, and with them came another man with a small white beard who appeared to be the grandfather of the children, and with him was a DOG! Oscar was beside himself with excitement. While the minks eyed the dog with a certain level of caution, Oscar excused himself from his friends and went straight into the water and swam out near the floats. Now all of the children, their parents, their grandfather, and the dog were on the float, and Oscar was sure the dog had spotted him since he started running back and forth on the float and barked up a storm.

Oscar was fascinated by this particular dog. He had never seen one quite like it on the boats in Heriot Bay. It could almost be an otter with its short legs and long slender body, but its nose was far too pointy, its whiskers far too short, and it did not have webbed feet. This last feature was a reassurance to Oscar, since he knew the dog could not swim as fast as he could and therefore did not pose a threat should he happen to jump into the water. The dog kept up his frantic running and barking until the grandfather called to him to be quiet, and this was the most amazing thing: the dog's name sounded just like "Oscar." Oscar was so astounded that he just floated in the water with his head out and stared.

After a while, the children put on their life jackets and made ready for their daily kayak paddle around the bay. Oscar was torn between joining them as usual and staying near the float to play more of his dog game. However, the grandfather went back up to the big house, taking the Oscar-dog with him, and this made the choice an easy one. This time, the children and their parents went out to the rocks where Oscar had seen his first seals, so he decided to tag along doing his usual tricks of swimming under the kayaks and popping his head up very close, making the children squeal with delight.

As they approached the rocks, Oscar had a strange feeling that everything was not quite right. He stopped playing for a moment and looked all around. Suddenly, he spotted something that made him not want to play around any more: sitting on the highest point of the seal rocks was a giant bald eagle that was looking straight at him. Oscar took a deep breath and dove as deep as he could and headed back toward his den. He made it in just three dives, a new record, and scrambled into his cozy den. As far as he could tell, the eagle had not even taken off after him, but he decided to stay in for the rest of the day, just to make sure. Besides, he had had a big lunch with his friends, a new dog had arrived, and all was right in his world. He slept very well until after dark and then ventured out for a midnight snack

"Suddenly, he spotted something that made
him not want to play ..."

Chapter four
Another Close Call

After the children and their parents left, things were a lot quieter in the bay, but the Oscar-dog would come down to the floats at least once a day and play with him, although from a distance and never in the water. It was all great fun, but Oscar did miss the children to show off for.

The really low tides were now in the middle of the day, so the clam-bed farmers were in the channel nearly every day tending the nets and harvesting clams and oysters. They brought their dog each time, but Oscar still could not lure him onto a float for a game. The Oscar-dog would come down to the channel and run around with the other dog, and they seemed to get along quite well, but Oscar knew better than to leave the water and try to play with them on the land.

One day, after the clam farmers had left on their boat and the tide had just started back in, Oscar decided to go over and check out the nets to see if there were any easy pickings. He found one corner of a net that had not been secured and was able to pull it back a bit so he could get his paw underneath and scrape away at the sand and rocks. There, just below the surface, he found more clams than he had ever imagined.

He began gorging himself on the delectable little morsels, all the while working his way bit by bit further under the net.

Finally, he had had his fill of clams and decided to go for a swim around the bay. The tide had really started to come in now, and he was in the water. As he tried to back out from under the net, one of his rear paws caught in the netting. He turned and twisted, trying to get free but just seemed to get himself more wound up.

The water was rising rather quickly now over the flat surface of the channel, and Oscar knew that he had to get free very quickly or he could drown. His mother's warning about the nets came back to him, and he wished he had remembered it earlier. Suddenly down the ramp to the channel came the Oscar-dog. When the dog spotted the otter in the nets, he set up a great barking. Oscar was worried that the dog might choose to attack him in his trapped condition, but the dog just kept up his frantic barking. Finally, the grandfather came down the ramp to see what all the noise was about and sized up the situation in an instant.

Oscar was getting pretty frantic himself at this point with the water rising all the time. The grandfather approached the otter very slowly speaking in low soft tones to try to calm him. He reached down carefully and unwound the net from Oscar's foot. When he felt it come free, Oscar made for the water's edge like a shot. When his heart had stopped pounding, he popped his head out of the water and looked back to the channel. He could see the grandfather waving to him and the Oscar-dog running around still barking, and he knew he was one very lucky otter.

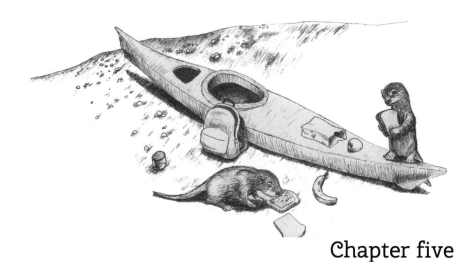

Chapter five
A Visit

Summer was now in full swing, and it was staying light until very late. Oscar and his friends would play for hours and go to sleep with a wonderful feeling of complete exhaustion. One day, Oscar spied a large group of kayakers heading toward the Breton Islands and decided it would be a good day to pay a visit to his sister, Octavia. He swam out quickly paying special attention to the seal rocks to make sure the eagle was not around. He made it to the Bretons before the kayakers and found his sister swimming around the rocks at the south end of the islands watching the seals there. The kayakers also came out to look at the seals and then pulled their craft up onto a little beach and went exploring on the largest of the islands.

Oscar motioned to Octavia to follow him, and they made their way to the beach where the kayaks were. There was no one around, so Oscar ventured out of the water and checked out the interiors of the kayaks. It did not take him long to find the knapsacks containing the kayakers' luncheon, and the siblings easily opened them. There were some jars and tins that the otters could not open, but the sandwiches were easily gotten into, and the fillings were quite tasty, especially the sardine and tuna ones. Oscar, of course, had to try everything but wished he had passed up the peanut butter. It took him the rest of the afternoon to get the sticky stuff off the roof of his mouth, and the taste stayed with him for several days.

The two otters heard the kayakers coming back just in time to make it into the water, leaving behind them quite a mess, and they paddled away to the dismayed sounds of the people who now had less than half the lunch they had planned on.

Oscar and Octavia decided to swim a little farther north to the rock chute they had discovered with their mother and brother the summer before. They found the otter whose territory included the chute and asked his permission to play for a while. He joined them, and they spent the next few hours sliding into the water and trying to see who could make the biggest splash. Oscar won that contest hands down.

Finally, it was time to leave, and they bid their friend goodbye and headed back to Octavia's den. They gave a wide berth to the beach where the kayakers had been, but they had all left, having had to clean up the rather large mess made by the two otters. The seals were still sunning themselves on the rocks, so the otters decided to join them. They watched as a shrimp boat came out to pull up its traps and pour the squirmy little pink shrimp into large coolers. Oscar had heard that shrimp were extremely good to eat, but they lived too deep in the water for him to dive to. He would just have to find some unattended bucket or cooler of them to sample, and he put this on his future "to do" list.

As the otters were lolling about on the rocks, they spotted a very big cruiser coming down the Hoskyn Channel. It turned toward Hyacinthe Bay as it passed the Bretons and appeared to be headed to the floats near Oscar's den. Octavia decided to stay in the warm sun, but Oscar just had to see where the big boat was going and if there was an opportunity for more mischief.

Chapter six
New Friends and Fun

Sure enough, the big cruiser made straight for the larger of the two floats by the little islet and proceeded to tie up. The grandfather and the Oscar-dog were down on the float to greet their new arrivals, and what should appear at the stern on the boat but another dog! The two dogs ran around each other on the float and seemed to be having such a good time that Oscar thought he might as well join in. He dove down and popped up right next to the float. The new dog did not seem to know what to make of this and backed away, but the Oscar-dog recognized him and barked out a greeting. After staying around for a little while and seeing that the new dog did not seem to get the idea of the dog game, Oscar swam back to his den for a bit of a nap; it had been a long day.

When it finally started to get dark, Oscar left his den to look for a light snack to finish up the day and to do something to get that peanut-butter taste out of his mouth. He swam over to the big cruiser to check it out and found, to his delight, several containers left out on the swim platform. All was dark on the boat, so he decided to hop out onto the platform and check out the buckets. One of them held half a dozen Dungeness crabs, and the other was about half-full of shrimp. Oscar could not believe his eyes! He did not know where to start, but he decided to try the shrimp first. They were delicious, and he downed about ten of them before he knew it.

Then Oscar moved to the crabs and flipped one out onto the swim platform. It tried to scramble away, but Oscar was on it in an instant and started to play with it before gobbling it down. This made quite a bit of noise and roused the dog on the boat, which finally found his bark. Lights came on in the cabin, the door to the afterdeck opened, and a man came out with a flashlight. He swung the light over the platform just as Oscar scrambled into the water and was able to see the mess the otter had made of his future dinner. It was obvious he was not happy at all and picked up both buckets and moved them into the boat, slamming the door.

Oscar figured that the man would not make the mistake of leaving buckets of tasty seafood out in plain sight again, but he had had his shrimp, and it was one extremely happy young otter that headed back to his den to sleep.

"He swung the light over the platform just as Oscar scrambled
into the water ..."

Chapter seven
Hitching a Ride

The big boat stayed tied up to the float for the next several days with people coming and going all of the time. The grandfather, who Oscar figured out must be the innkeeper his mother had told him about, and a very pretty lady came down from the big house frequently with the Oscar-dog and would join the people on the boat to dig clams and gather oysters. He noticed that when the people took their buckets of clams and oysters back to the boat they did not leave them on the swim platform. Of course, this did not bother Oscar at all since both of those shellfish were so easy to come by. He did miss the shrimp and crabs, though.

One day, the people on the boat said they would be leaving the next day to head around Read Island on their way to a place they called Desolation Sound. Oscar remembered how his father had told him about getting to faraway places by sneaking onto large boats' swim platforms. He knew that this particular boat would be a challenge because they had a dog and they did not have a platform with lots of things tied on, which could be used as hiding places. However, he thought that perhaps he would try just a short ride to see his brother, Omar, on the other side of Read Island. It was a long swim, but it would take only a short time on the back of this big cruiser. He could then take his time coming back and even stop off to see Octavia on the way home.

Oscar got up very early the next morning and swam over to the floats. He got under the one not being used by the cruiser and stayed very quiet. Pretty soon, there was a lot of activity around the boat with the people and the dogs all saying their goodbyes. When the lines were cast off the float, the big cruiser backed slowly away. Just as it turned to head off around the little islet, Oscar made a short dash and hopped right out of the water onto the swim platform. Neither the people nor the dog on the boat were any the wiser that they had a hitchhiker on board, but the innkeeper and the pretty lady were on the float still and saw what had happened. Oscar could see that they were laughing, but they did not yell to the people on the boat, so he stayed on his perch.

Luckily, the man driving the boat was not in a big hurry, so the ride was fairly smooth, but Oscar knew that for any longer trip he would need to have something to hide under to protect himself from the wake of the cruiser and to keep from being seen. As they motored slowly out past the Bretons, Oscar saw Octavia on the rocks by the seals, and he waved to her. She just stared at him in utter amazement until the boat disappeared around the tip of Read Island.

On board, Oscar watched the shoreline pass by until he spotted the cove where Omar had his den. He was just about ready to jump ship when the skipper decided to speed up. Oscar was nearly thrown right off the platform but recovered himself enough to make a somewhat graceful exit. He hit the water pretty hard and filed that away for future reference—remember to get off at slow speed.

Oscar swam into Omar's cove and found his brother sitting in the doorway of his den, where he had witnessed Oscar's nosedive off the stern of the cruiser. They had a good laugh about it, and then Omar showed him around.

The two brothers had a great visit and hunted and explored together for a couple of days. When Oscar said he thought he should be getting back to his own den, Omar promised to come over for a while and told Oscar that the next time he came to Read Island they would go over and explore parts of Cortes Island. Omar had covered the western shore and found some interesting places that would be fun for the two of them. Oscar was always up for a new adventure and promised to return before the end of the summer.

On the way back to his own den, Oscar stopped by to see Octavia, and she told him how shocked she had been at seeing him on the back of the boat. He told her it was grand fun but omitted that part about his very unceremonious departure from the swim platform. He knew she would hear it soon enough from Omar. When he finally made it home, he was very tired and realized just how far a swim it was. He went to sleep dreaming of further travels, like his father made, and wondered where the next one would take him.

Chapter eight
More Mischief

Oscar spent the next few days resting up from his trip to Read Island. He was still nursing a bit of a sore shoulder from his tumble off the back of the big cruiser. He had lunch with his friends on the beach and played with the Oscar-dog when he came down to the float, but mostly he just ate, slept, and paddled around Hyacinthe Bay.

One day at high tide, when there was a lot of water in the channel, he swam back to the small bay below the big house. He had not spent much time there at all, so he did a little exploring of the area. He could see that there were some more nets on the bottom of the bay and knew there had to be clams there. He could also see oysters and spotted a couple of small rock crabs. He knew the crabs were tasty but not as fantastic as the Dungeness one he had grabbed off the big boat. All in all, it looked like a good place for a change of pace for a meal, but he did note that there were several tall craggy trees around the bay, which were favorite places for eagles, so he knew he would need to be careful.

He looked up at the inn on the hill and decided to check it out. He remembered how the Oscar-dog and the innkeeper had saved his life when he had been caught in the clam net in the channel so he figured they meant him no harm. However, he realized that he was now in the dog's territory so he would have to watch his step, just as his mother had taught him. The one thing his mother could never teach him, though, was to control his youthful enthusiasm and curiosity.

Oscar left the water and scrambled over the driftwood and up the hill to the house. He noticed that there was another little house next to the main inn, and he decided to approach from the side rather than the front. There was a stairway up to a deck, so he moved quietly up and peered across the deck. He could see there was another very large deck in front of the main inn as well, and off at the far end, he could see the Oscar-dog stretched out in the warm sun, sound asleep. He ventured further onto the deck, keeping his eye on the dog, and surveyed the scene. All of the doors of the inn were open onto the deck, and he could hear some music coming from inside. He also smelled something VERY good coming from the first door and simply HAD to find out what it was.

Still being very quiet, he peeked in the door. No one was around, the dog was still sleeping, the music was playing softly, and his curiosity was simply too much—he had to go inside. Once inside, he found there were even more great smells of things being cooked, and he suddenly found himself hungry.

All of the countertops were too high for him to see what was on them, but a stool had been pulled out at the end of one of them. Ever so slowly, he crept across the floor and raised himself up on the stool. He then put his paws on the counter and peered over the top. There was an array of food, which he did not recognize, but he knew must be good, and after all, he WAS hungry.

Just as he was reaching out for something that looked particularly tasty, he heard a noise behind him and turned just in time to see the innkeeper come into the far end of the room. The man yelled at him, and Oscar wheeled and fell off the stool, tipping it over in the process. It crashed to the floor along with the otter, and this was enough to wake up the dog. He could hear the scampering feet coming but was out the door and off across the deck the way he had come in with the dog in hot pursuit. He knew that this was no time to try to make friends since he had invaded the other animal's territory, so he made a mad dash to the water and swam out into the bay. The dog did not try to follow him down to the water but stayed up on the hill, barking.

Oscar could see the innkeeper out on the deck looking at him, and he seemed to be smiling. He waved to the otter just as he had done when he had seen him climb onto the cruiser's swim platform, and Oscar decided that he did not have anything to fear from him, but he sensed that it might be different for the dog who had had his turf violated. Oscar knew that any future visits would have to be made cautiously, but he was tempted by the wonderful smells coming from that room and felt compelled to return to find out what the tastes were that went with them.

Chapter nine
More Newcomers

Oscar stayed away from the inn for a while after his adventure and contented himself with the bay, the floats, and the area around his den. The Oscar-dog still came down to the floats every day to play and seemed to have forgotten all about the incident.

A few days later, more excitement entered his world. A whole group of young adults arrived and brought a new boat down to the floats. This was not a big cruiser, but the people used it to pull each other around the bay on an assortment of strange-looking devices. They seemed to be having a grand time laughing and shouting among themselves and even seemed to like it when they fell off whatever devices they were on and went into the water with a huge splash. Oscar remembered his tumble from the stern of the cruiser and could not understand why these people thought it was so much fun.

The boat, with its cargo in tow, moved very quickly and changed directions constantly, so Oscar made sure to give it a wide berth when he was in the water. Every once in a while, though, two of the younger of the boys in the group would take the boat out without the others and go fishing. They went much slower, and he was able to swim around them and perform his usual antics. The boys seemed to like having him along and would occasionally throw small fish they caught into the water for Oscar to grab. He did not mind at all having someone else do his hunting for him, so he joined in this game with delight.

This group was so loud and lively that his friends the minks and the deer did not want to come out to the beach on the little islet for their usual lunch meetings. Instead, they moved to the beach in the bay below the inn. There were guests staying at the inn who would come out onto the big deck to watch the four of them and would be very quiet, allowing them a peaceful meal. With so many people around, Oscar was not able to pay a return visit to the good-smelling room, but with everything else going on, he did not mind too much. He knew he would be back.

The group of young people stayed about a week, and by the time they left, Oscar could smell in the air a change of season approaching. Most of the boats he could see out in the Sutil and Hoskyn Channels were now headed south, and he could tell summer was coming to an end. The weather still stayed warm and sunny, so there was plenty to do with his friends, and he had a few areas close to home left to explore.

However, he remembered his brother's proposal to do some exploring of Cortes Island and thought it would be best to do that before storms began coming into the area. So one day, Oscar tidied up his den, had a special lunch with his friends, told them where he was going, and headed off to Omar's den. He stopped and spent the night with Octavia in the Bretons on the way, and they filled each other in on their adventures since they had last been together. It had been an eventful summer for both, and it was fun to catch up. In the morning, he said goodbye to Octavia and paddled around the end of Read Island and up the shore to Omar's cove.

Chapter ten
Cortes Island

Omar was very excited to see Oscar, especially when he heard the reason for his visit. He insisted that they start off right away so they could make it to Whaletown before dark. Omar told Oscar that Whaletown was where the ferry from Heriot Bay came to on Cortes and there were docks, dogs, beaches, and plenty of good hunting. Oscar told Omar of his adventures with the two boys who caught fish for him, but Omar doubted they would have a lot of luck with that where they were going.

They grabbed a quick bite in Omar's cove before paddling across the Sutil Channel toward Whaletown. They arrived in the small harbor just as the ferry from Quadra Island was arriving. They both stayed away from the churning currents around the propellers of the ferry, but even at a distance, they could feel the strength of the eddies and remembered their mother's warning about the dock in Heriot Bay. When the ferry had safely tied up at its dock, they crossed the harbor and explored the tiny marina. There was not much going on, but Oscar did find a dog on the dock to victimize, and both he and Omar had a good laugh.

They waited until the ferry left for its return trip to Heriot Bay and then continued south along the shore. They came to a vast shallows right off what Omar said was Marina Island, but he showed Oscar where there was a tight channel that boats could use even at low tide to pass between the two islands.

It was starting to get dark, and the tide was still going out, so Omar suggested that they have a meal of clams that abounded in the shallows and then spend the night on some uninhabited rocks near the channel. Omar explained there was another very special place he wanted to show his brother, but they needed to wait until a slack tide, and it would be safest to make this part of the journey in the daylight.

Morning dawned bright and clear, and as soon as the tide stopped running and went slack, the brothers started off together, with Omar in the lead. When they came around one of the large rocks, Omar showed Oscar a tiny opening in the shoreline on Cortes Island. They swam through the narrow passage that opened up into a spacious area Omar said was called Gorge Harbor. There were several small islands inside the bay and even quite a large marina with a number of boats tied up at its docks. However, the best part Omar pointed out were the floats where someone was farming mussels and oysters. They both remembered fondly the easy pickings they had discovered with their mother and sister in Crescent Channel behind Bold Island the summer before and decided to explore the bay a bit before returning for their evening meal.

The brothers had a grand time together and even found a few children to show off for at the resorts on the shores of the bay. They stayed several days and explored every last cove inside Gorge Harbor. They also found enough things to get into on the swim platforms of the boats in the marina and on the docks of the resorts to leave quite a mess and let everyone know they had been there.

At last, Oscar felt it was time to get back to his own den and thanked his brother for such a fun adventure. They took their time getting back home, and Omar even came with Oscar to visit Octavia at her place. They had a good time telling her of their discoveries and mischief, and she asked if she could join them the next time they made the trek. They readily agreed, and then the boys headed off to their respective dens.

Chapter eleven
Home Sweet Home

Oscar swam up to his cozy little den and settled down for a good sleep. He had been on the go for days, and his own bed was very comforting. Besides, there were many potential adventures right here, and he was not going to miss a one. As he dropped off to sleep, the smells from the big room up at the inn came back to him, and he closed his eyes to the lullaby of a growling stomach.

Ahh … there was so much to do …

THE STORY CONTINUES

Book Three

The First Big Trip

Chapter one
Fall Fun

The weather continued warm and sunny, but Oscar knew that fall was on the way. There were fewer boats out in the channels, and most of them were on the move south, back to their winter homes. However, Oscar now knew that, come spring, they would be back, and he looked forward to playing with the children and dogs. In the meantime, he had his friends the mink and the deer, and the Oscar-dog was still around for play.

One morning when he emerged from his den, he heard a rustling in the area behind him. He turned around and spotted a young raccoon coming down to the water's edge. He remembered him from the raccoon family he had come across right after he had moved into his den. Oscar now realized this young one was out on his own and not under the protective eye of its mother that had been so inhospitable to Oscar when he had tried to approach her family.

It seemed as good a time as any to make a new friend, so Oscar hailed the raccoon. They hit it off right away and became fast friends so Oscar took him to meet the minks and deer at their next lunch together. The minks were not quite sure what to make of the raccoon at first, but after a while, they warmed to him and welcomed him into their little group. They swapped stories as they lolled around on the beach of the islet, and the raccoon had quite a few tales of mischief he and his siblings had gotten into around the docks at the marina in Heriot Bay. The minks and the deer were not into the sort of tricks he told of, being much shier, but Oscar was all ears.

The raccoon told of the grocery cart that people from the market up the hill would bring down to the boats and how much fun it was to get into it if it was left unattended, which would happen sometimes at very low tides when the ramp down to the docks was at too steep an angle for the delivery boy to get it down. The boy would grab a few bags at a time and walk down to the boats, returning as many times as it took to empty the cart. In-between, the raccoon and his brother would slip up and grab a few items from a bag in the cart and make off with them. If the delivery boy made several trips, they could get away with quite a stash of tasty food.

The people on the boats would always notice that some things were missing and send the boy back to the market to get replacements. This did not make the boy very happy since he had to go back and ask for the items, and he would always get in trouble. However, the young raccoons always had a good laugh and a great meal at the boy's expense. Oscar, always in the mood for free food, offered to join in the next time they were going to make a raid, and the raccoon set it up for the very next day.

The raccoon and his brother came down to the docks by land, but Oscar swam down from his den and met them in some bushes near the top of the ramp to the dock. The tide was far out, and the ramp was much too steep for the delivery boy to take the cart down it if he had a delivery to make.

They did not have to wait long. Several of the boats that were leaving on their way south were stocking up for the trip, and the boy came with a cart filled to the top with bags of groceries. It took him half a dozen trips to get them all down to the dock, and Oscar and the two raccoons had quite a pile of food by the time he was finished.

Everyone who had a delivery was missing something, and each insisted that the boy go back for the missing items. When he came up the ramp, he was not in a very good mood. As he was turning the cart around for his trip back up to the market, he noticed a package of sugar doughnuts that one of the raccoons had dropped in his hurry to get back into the bushes. A little farther away, the boy spied another item from one of the bags, and he began to follow the trail. The three food filchers saw him coming and decided to make a break for it with as much as they could carry. The boy was very close when the three of them burst from the bushes. He let out a yell and jumped back in surprise.

The two raccoons were able to make it to the cover of some nearby woods with a good portion of their loot, but Oscar headed back down to the water and the way he had come. He did have a large bag of bread in his mouth, but when he dove into the water, it got all wet and turned to mush, so he did not get to enjoy it. The prank, however, was all worth it as far as Oscar was concerned, and he swam back to his den in a good mood.

The boy went back up to the market and told the owners what had happened at the docks, and they now understood that the missing items really were not the boy's fault, so he was not in trouble any more, which made him happy. The storeowners changed their routine after that so that when the tide was really low, they would send two delivery boys down with the cart. One could stand guard while the other made the deliveries.

This brought an end to the raccoons' game and supply of free food, which did not make them very happy, but they had enjoyed the prank as much as Oscar had and decided to get together with him to devise some new schemes for mischief.

"The three food filchers saw him coming and decided to make a
break for it …"

Chapter two
Return to the Inn

A couple of days after the adventure at the docks, the two raccoons showed up at Oscar's den, and the three of them had a pleasant afternoon gathering shellfish and making up games to play in the woods and on the beach. The raccoons could swim, but nothing like Oscar, so they were not able to play any of the games that Oscar had with his siblings, but they had a good time, anyway.

As the afternoon wore on, the raccoons asked if there was any good mischief they could get into. Oscar thought immediately of the room with the wonderful smells at the inn on the hill but was not quite sure that he wanted to share his discovery with anyone else. However, he decided that with three of them, they might have a better chance of getting away with some of the goodies if one or two could provide a distraction for the innkeeper and the dog, so he presented his idea to the raccoons.

The raccoons had been near the inn before, but the dog had always been somewhere around and would start barking if he spotted them, so they had not even ventured onto the deck as Oscar had. They all determined that it was as good a time as any at least to take a look around and come up with a plan, so they started off toward the inn.

They approached the same way Oscar had on his previous visit. They crept up the stairs at the end of the deck and peered over the top. The dog was nowhere to be seen, but just as they peeked up, they saw the innkeeper come out of the big room that Oscar had told them about with the wondrous smells. He carried a large pan and put it on a table, surrounded by chairs, on the deck.

The pretty lady came out of the house, also, and the two people sat down at the table. Just as they did, a bell rang inside the house, and they both went inside. The trio hiding on the stairs could hear them talking inside and made their way across the small deck onto the large one and over to the table. One of them kept an eye out for the dog and the people while the other two made their way onto the chairs and looked over the table. Oscar could see that the pan was full of clams and that they had already been opened. He thought this would be the easiest feast they had ever had and reached out to grab a clam. So did the raccoon that was with him.

In snatching a clam, both of them touched the side of the very hot pan and let out a loud yelp. They dropped their clams and scrambled down from the chairs just as the two people came back out onto the deck. All the innkeeper and the pretty lady saw were three furry bodies racing across the deck and into the woods, but it was obvious what had happened. The two people were laughing and sat back down to enjoy their clams. The three potential thieves could only watch from the bushes, with two of them sucking on a sore paw.

The Oscar-dog finally came out onto the deck, yawning and stretching, and was completely unaware of what had happened. The raccoons thought it would be fun to get the dog to run around and bark so they made a lot of noise in the bushes to attract his attention. He came running down to the end of the deck by the stairs where the three of them had come up, and he could get their scent but could not see them in the bushes. He barked a lot, though, and the innkeeper finally came over and told him to be quiet and led him back up to the big deck.

Oscar stayed completely out of sight; he had been caught once already and thought it would be best to let the raccoons be the ones to take the blame if they were spotted. The three made their way quietly back to Oscar's den and had a good laugh and talked about making another trip to the inn.

Chapter Three
News from Home

A few days after his adventure with the raccoon brothers at the inn, Oscar's paw began to feel better, and he emerged from his den as hungry as he could remember ever being. He made straight for the channel to go after some clams and oysters and found the two minks already there. They enjoyed a real feast, and finally the minks excused themselves since they could not hold another bite.

Oscar stayed on for a bit to polish off a few more clams, and just as he was ready to leave, around the corner of the little islet, came his mother and her two new kits. She had been training them for the past several months and had not had time to check in on Oscar. They had a pleasant visit, and he enjoyed showing off for his new brother and sister.

As Mother and the new brood were ready to leave, she mentioned to Oscar that his father would be coming back to the area in a little while. Oscar was very excited to hear this and was looking forward to more tales of his father's travels. Mother told him that she would be sure to tell Father to visit Oscar at his new home and then took the two new youngsters back to her den.

Oscar went back to his den and set about making it VERY tidy in anticipation of his father's return. He was also excited since he had a few travel tales of his own to share with Father and knew they would have a grand time.

The weather grew cooler, and one day he noticed that he had not seen the Oscar-dog in a few days. He made a quick trip up to the inn to look for him and found all of the doors onto the big deck closed. There was no sign of the innkeeper, the pretty lady, or the dog, and Oscar had a moment of sadness at the loss of their company. Of course, most of the sadness was caused by the realization that any more raids on the room with the wonderful smells would have to wait until they came back, whenever that might be. He still had his friends, but he would miss teasing the dog. He also thought he could still get into some mischief with the raccoon brothers, but they would now have to go a little farther in search of objects for their pranks.

The first storms had now begun to arrive, and it got quite cold very early in the season. There were even a few flurries but not enough to provide any real playing in snow. One day, the raccoons came by his den to tell him they might not see him very often for a while. They explained that although they didn't really hibernate, as bears do, they did go somewhat dormant if the weather got really cold. They promised to come by whenever they were out foraging, but again Oscar felt a twinge of sadness thinking about not seeing his friends as often.

So, Oscar settled into a much more relaxed routine of getting together with the minks and deer on a regular basis and keeping his den in fine order for the visit of his father. The weeks passed, and it got colder and colder. The snow came in earnest, and even a portion of Hyacinthe Bay froze over, so he was able to play on the ice and taught the minks how to slide across it and make spectacular crashes into banks of snow. The three of them had great fun, but the deer chose not to get involved after the first time he tried to walk on the ice and fell down very hard.

One evening, which came quite early now, after a long period of ice-play with the minks, Oscar came back to his den to find his father perched at his front door. Oscar was very excited and invited his father inside right away. They shared a meal of special treats Oscar had saved up for the occasion and settled into telling stories. It was getting light outside when they finally realized that they were so tired they could hardly keep their eyes open. They both stretched out and slept for a very long time.

Chapter four
A Plan Emerges

F ather stayed around for almost a week, and he and Oscar had a marvelous time. Oscar told of his adventures, including his ride on the boat and visit with Omar and their exploration of the western shore of Cortes Island.

Father told Oscar of the other side of Cortes where there were wonderful harbors and trails. He encouraged Oscar to get his brother and sister to make the trip around the south end of the island and up the eastern side stopping at Cortes Bay and Squirrel Cove. He told him of a fascinating trail leading from one part of Squirrel Cove over to Von Donop Inlet.

He also described a tiny passage at the end of Squirrel Cove that led to a bay inside the island, which had a little island in it. Father said it was great fun to ride the currents of the channel during changes in the tide. Oscar was extremely excited about the prospect of sharing this adventure with his siblings and made a note to talk to Omar and Octavia about it at the first opportunity.

However, Father had another plan in mind for his young son and let him in on it one evening. He told him he would like to take him up to the Octopus Islands at the far north end of Quadra Island. Oscar remembered his father's stories of this beautiful area and could not wait to go. His father explained it was a rather dangerous journey since to get there they would have to traverse either Hole-in-the-Wall or Surge Narrows. The latter was by far the shortest route but the most tricky due to the fast-running tidal currents. The passage was also very narrow, and there were many whirlpools that could actually suck them under if they got caught in one. The best way for them to get there was to hitch a ride on a boat, but that would also be difficult since there were not many pleasure craft about at this time of year.

Oscar was so excited about this possibility that his father said he would go off to see if he could pick up any information about boats headed through the narrows in the next few weeks. He told Oscar to stick around his den and be ready to leave at a moment's notice, and he left the next morning to look for a ride north.

Oscar's father had been gone for nearly two weeks, and Oscar thought perhaps he had forgotten him until very early one morning he was roughly awakened by his father shaking him and telling him they would have to leave right now and swim very hard and fast. His father had heard that the men who worked at the fish farm out near Octavia's den were headed up through the narrows and would be towing a small float. With the float in tow, they had to make the passage at dead slack tide, which was not very far off.

They swam as fast as they could and reached the fish farm just as the men were loading their boat. The small float was already tied to the boat, and Oscar and his father concealed themselves among the timbers as quickly and quietly as they could. The men were busy and did not notice the arrival of their passengers. Oscar and his father held their breaths as the boat's motor started and it pulled away from the farm, keeping the little float on a short line and a lot closer to the boat than they liked.

The run up between Quadra and Read Islands to the narrows went relatively quickly, but it seemed like a very long time to Oscar and his father. Finally, they could hear a change in the speed of the boat's motor and knew they were getting close. They picked up a little speed and could see that the men had missed dead slack. It was not by much, but the tidal currents had already begun to change, and they held on for what promised to be an interesting ride. They could see some whirlpools off to the side, and the men pulled the line on the float in even tighter, but they were so busy they did not notice the stowaways.

They were just a little over halfway through the narrows when the boat suddenly changed direction sharply to avoid a large floating log in the channel. The little float played a game of crack-the-whip with the boat, nearly throwing both otters into the churning waters. They dug their claws into the timbers and succeeded in hanging on, just barely.

After what seemed like forever, the water started to smooth out, and they knew they had made it through. At this point, Father motioned to Oscar, and they made a hasty exit from their ride, swimming under water and not surfacing until they were clear of the boat and the fish farmers by a good margin.

The two otters smiled at each other in relief and proceeded on to the Octopus Islands at a leisurely pace, stopping here and there to do a bit of fishing.

Chapter five
Octopus Islands

When they reached the islands, Oscar was delighted to discover them to be every bit as beautiful as his father had described, even in the winter. There was not a single pleasure boat in the marine park; they had the place to themselves.

There were three main islands and many small ones to explore, plus the wonderful little coves and harbors, which, Father explained, were filled with boats during the summer months. He told Oscar he had picked up many a ride with cruisers here and he could pick and choose his direction.

The largest harbor was very shallow, and its mouth was protected by a number of rocks that lay just below the surface. Father told Oscar that he had seen many a boat go aground on these rocks, sometimes more than one at a time. He said that the boaters were quite amusing to watch trying everything to get off the rocks and all the while looking very embarrassed in front of all of the other people moored in the harbor. Usually several boats would launch their dinghies and lend a hand in pulling the stranded boats off the rocks, but sometimes they just had to wait for the tide to come in to float them off.

The two otters explored the bottom of the main harbor, and it was here that Oscar saw his first octopus. He found it utterly fascinating as it sort of flowed across the bottom in an undulating motion with its eight legs spread out. Oscar could have watched it for hours if he could have held his breath that long. At one point, Oscar took a deep breath and dove down to get a closer look at the strange creature, but as soon as he got close, the octopus expelled a large cloud of black ink and disappeared from view. When the water finally cleared a bit, Oscar spotted the shy octopus with its entire body compressed into a bundle in a tiny crack in the rocks. Try as he might, Oscar could not get him to come out and had to move on to other explorations.

Father and son spent the better part of a week swimming around the small islands and through the narrow channels between them. Food was abundant, and they had no trouble filling their tummies. One evening just before it got dark, they came upon a tiny cove on one of the three main islands and swam into it. Father sensed something very strange and told his son to follow his lead. He rolled on his back and just lay in the water not moving a muscle, and Oscar joined him.

What they experienced was truly magical. Without their moving at all, the gentle tidal current swept them into the cove for a bit and then gently reversed, pulling them back out toward the entrance again. Just about when it seemed as if they would float out into the channel, the current would reverse, and they would gently ride it back into the cove. This kept up for about half an hour; it was almost as if they were being rocked to sleep by the water. Then, just as suddenly as it had started, it stopped. The two of them just looked at each other in amazement. Father said he had never experienced that before and had no explanation, but they both agreed that the sensation was something they would not soon forget.

While they were swimming around one of the larger islands one day, they noticed a small cabin on shore that looked abandoned. Since there was absolutely no one around, they decided to look inside. The windows no longer had glass in them, and the front door was missing, so they just walked in. What they saw was one of the strangest things Oscar could possibly imagine. Apparently, the summer boaters would come ashore here and each put a token of their visit up on the walls or hang it from the rafters. There was every sort of collection of driftwood, sea shells, rocks, pieces of rope or chain, broken items off the boats, and just about anything else you could think of. Some of the collections had been connected with nails, screws, wire, rope, or fishing line, and some had the things suspended from pieces of wire or fishing line and were hung up on the rafters so they would swing gently in the breeze.

"What they saw was one of the strangest things Oscar could possibly imagine."

Oscar's father had visited this cabin once several years before and told him that it looked as if people had been adding things every year since there was a lot more than he remembered. Neither of them could figure out just why the people would gather such strange items and put them in the cabin, but they decided just to leave it as a mystery. They did not disturb a single odd item and left quite bewildered.

One day, Oscar's father announced he was going to be moving on and Oscar should start making his way back to his den. The older otter was headed farther west down the main channel to pick up a ride north. The two of them swam out of the Octopus Islands and across the Okisollo Channel to the mouth of what Father called Hole-in-the-Wall. Father took quite a bit of time to show his son how to navigate this stretch of water and make his way back home. They found a good-size log, stuck in some rocks on the shore at the entrance to Hole-in-the-Wall, and freed it but kept it on land so it did not float away. Father told Oscar to wait until the tide changed in the channel and then simply ride the log all they way through to the other side, which emptied into Calm Channel.

Father said he would wait to tell Oscar exactly the time to leave and, as soon as he exited Hole-in-the-Wall, he should turn right down Calm Channel. He gave Oscar the landmarks to look for to find Whiterock Passage, which would take him back to Hoskyn Channel and home. Oscar paid close attention to his father since he knew this would be a long and possibly dangerous journey and his first really big solo adventure. He was very pleased that his father had so much faith in him to trust him to find his way home all alone.

Before long, Oscar could see that the water direction was changing. His father told him it was time to go and helped him push the log out into the current. Oscar hopped on, the two waved goodbye, and he was on his way—to what, he was not quite sure.

Chapter six
Really Big Water

The ride through Hole-in-the-Wall was like nothing Oscar had ever experienced. At the mouth where he had entered, it was quite narrow, but as he and his log moved along, it opened up into a wide channel. He thought that the speed of the current would decrease as the passage widened, but quite the opposite occurred. The passage narrowed again, briefly, about three-quarters of the way through and then opened up again, but all of the time, the speed of the current kept increasing. When he finally reached the end of the passage, he was traveling far faster than he could ever swim, and the current launched him and his log right out into Calm Channel, which indeed was calm, especially compared to his wild ride through Hole-in-the-Wall.

His father had told him to turn right as soon as he exited the passage and head down along the shore of Maurelle Island until he came to the first real channel, which would lead him to Whiterock Passage and the way to his home. However, as he sat on his log in the middle of this now-peaceful water, he heard off in the distance to his left a strange rushing sound and decided to see what it was. As he ventured further north, the rushing sound turned into a roar.

The water where he was remained relatively calm, but he knew the sound had to be that of a lot of water moving very quickly. The channel made a bend to the right, and Oscar saw the most amazing sight. Up ahead, where the channel narrowed only slightly, there was a solid wall of water about three feet high all the way across it. The wall looked like a wave, but it was just staying in one place and not moving either toward or away from him. He could see some giant whirlpools near the wave and was pretty sure he did not want to get much closer.

Then he remembered his father telling him about the Yuculta Rapids and knew this must be the place. Father had told him of seeing a very large cruiser try to pass through the rapids when they were running and being thrown around like a woodchip by the churning currents. He could not imagine what they could do to him and his little log, but he could feel that it would not be very pleasant, even if it was exciting.

Oscar knew he would come back to this place in the future but would have to talk with his father about how to get through the rapids to the fascinating islands and marinas and small coves and strange wildlife in the area past the rapids, but that was going to have to wait until later.

With a sigh, Oscar turned his little log around and paddled back toward the exit of Hole-in-the-Wall and then down the shore of the island where he could see the entrance of another channel, which had to be Whiterock. Here he decided to part company with his faithful log that had seen him through his journey thus far and swam on his own. Whiterock Passage was very shallow and calm, and Oscar found it quite beautiful, even in the grayness of the winter. The water was crystal clear, and the bottom was visible as a jumble of smooth, round rocks. Long kelp grew up from between the rocks and swayed in the gentle current like young trees in a soft wind. It was very peaceful, and Oscar paddled slowly so as not to miss a thing. He came out into a little bay and swam along its shore.

A small group of islands off to his right seemed faintly familiar. As he got closer, he recognized them as the entrance to Surge Narrows that he and his father had traversed on the small float with the fish farmers, and he knew he was close to home. He knew he could probably make it home in a few hours, but a memory of the oyster and mussel farm in

Crescent Channel behind Bold Island came back to him, and he opted for one more night on his journey. He even found the same abandoned den he and his mother and siblings had used in their first trip here, and it seemed warm and inviting.

He swam over to the floats laden with the tasty shellfish and helped himself to a grand meal. He did not even mind that he had no one to share it with. When he had eaten far more than he should have, he paddled very slowly back to the old den and settled in for the night. Before he dropped off to sleep, he made up his mind to stop by and see his sister in the Bretons before returning to his own den. He just HAD to tell someone about his wonderful adventure.

Chapter seven
Reunion

After his long swim and huge meal, Oscar slept quite late, at least for him. He finally awoke to the almost-prehistoric call of a great blue heron that was fishing in the shallows of the calm channel. He never ceased to be intrigued by how such a gentle bird could have such a frightening call. Then he mused about the rather silly squeak of the bald eagle and how it contrasted with the strong, sharp talons and savage beak that could do so much harm to small creatures like otters. He decided that this was not a subject on which he would like to ponder, so he instead thought about his plan to visit his sister.

It was an easy paddle down the channel to Octavia's den in the Bretons. With each stroke, he became more excited with the prospect of sharing his adventures with her. When he rounded the corner of the little cove in which Octavia had her den, he was greeted by the sight of both Octavia and Omar splashing in the water. They were equally excited about seeing their brother, and they all started telling each other stories at once. When at last they all ran out of breath, they decided that it would probably be best if just one of them spoke at a time. They then settled in to relating their respective adventures since the last time they were together. Of course, Oscar could top them both with his tales of his travels with their father and, especially, the last leg of the journey, which he had managed on his own.

When they had finished telling their tales, it was quite late, so Octavia invited her brothers to stay the night. They were delighted to do so and became aware that Octavia had enlarged her den and made it extremely cozy. The night passed quickly, and the three siblings rose to a beautiful winter morning with chilly air and water but bright sunshine, which reflected on the small droplets of water that had frozen on the boughs of the trees along the shore. It appeared as if someone had hung lights on the trees, and the otters were amazed at the sight.

After a meal of fish from the cove, Oscar gathered his brother and sister and shared some of the information Father had imparted to him about future travels.

Chapter eight
Future Travels

Oscar reminded them of his trip with Omar to Gorge Harbor on Cortes Island earlier in the year and went on to relate Father's tales of places to see on the other side of the island. There was some talk of starting off on the adventure immediately, but Oscar was rather tired from his recent journey, and he prevailed upon them to wait until spring. He explained that there might be a few boats in the moorages if they waited, and that could provide additional opportunity for rides and mischief. This prospect carried the day, and all three started planning.

They agreed to wait until the first kayakers came out to Octavia's place since that would herald the return of more people and boats. Oscar could observe them from his den and then go out to the Bretons, gather up his sister, and head off to Omar's to commence the journey.

With this plan firmly in each of their minds, Oscar bid them farewell and swam off for his own den, which he knew would require a little housekeeping after his long absence. He had been impressed with the way Octavia had fixed up her place and was determined to make his just as nice.

Chapter nine
Winter Chores

On the way to his den, Oscar stopped in to see the two minks and found them well and pleased to have their friend back in the area. They told him they saw their friend the young deer frequently but the two raccoons had not been around for a while. Oscar told them of the raccoons' going into a dormant semi-hibernation state and they would be around only if they happened to be out foraging for food. With the subject of food coming up, the three of them adjourned to the beach for a brief snack.

With his belly now full, Oscar was ready to take on the task of putting his home in order. He found it in better shape than he had imagined it might be, and this relieved him greatly. In fact, he was SO relieved that he curled up to take a bit of a nap before starting work. When he awoke, it was dark, so he put off the work until the next day and went back to sleep.

When he arose the next morning, he found that the work had not been done while he slept, so he sighed and set about the business at hand. He first decided to make his den larger, as Octavia had done, so he could accommodate overnight guests. He dug farther back in his den, and suddenly, his paw went right through the back wall. He could hear a splashing sound and realized it was the gentle lapping of the waves against the rocks on the bay. He enlarged the opening and crawled in. He could see light coming through a crevice in the rock walls of this tunnel he had discovered and moved farther in toward the crack. It was large enough for him to enter. He wriggled through and found himself out on the water close to the floats and the beach where he had lunch with his friends.

This was an exciting discovery. It meant he had a secret entrance to his den AND he therefore had an emergency exit, should he ever need it. He decided right away not to share his secret with anyone, at least for now, and he set about gathering pieces of driftwood to conceal the entrance even better than it had been. This done, he returned through the secret passage to his den and concealed that end of the tunnel.

Oscar expanded his den off to the side of his discovery to provide the extra space he wanted and then went out to gather moss to line his new room. When he finished, he had a spacious den, which was most confortable.

Chapter ten
The Wait till Spring

With his new cozy den, Oscar was ready to take it easy for the next month or two by playing with his friends, eating, and sleeping. The minks and deer were frequent companions, and the raccoons even came by a few times when they were not sleeping themselves.

The innkeeper, the pretty lady, and the Oscar-dog even came back for a visit, but they were not outside much, and the doors to the big deck stayed closed most of the time so he could not get into the room with the wonderful smells. He did, however, find at least one new game to play. It turned out that the Oscar-dog had his bed inside, in front of one of the doors opening out onto the big deck. He would lie there most of the day, sleeping. Oscar would come up onto the deck when no one was around and creep up by the window in the door by the dog's bed. He would scratch at the window and duck down when the dog would start to stir. He would do this several times until he was sure the dog was awake and then pop his face up right in front of the window. The dog would leap up and start a frantic barking. Oscar would scamper away before either of the humans would come, but he could still hear the dog barking.

Oscar was sad when the people and the Oscar-dog left, but the days were starting to get longer and warmer, and he knew spring was not far off. Finally, when the leaves were returning to the trees and the robins and finches were much more plentiful, Oscar swam out into Hyacinthe Bay one day and spotted a group of kayakers headed towards the Bretons.

He knew the time had come, so he put his den in order, said goodbye to his friends, and set off for Octavia's and the beginning of a new adventure.

MORE FUN IN STORE

BOOK FOUR

A New Stage In Life

Chapter one
A Sibling Adventure

All winter, Oscar had been waiting to start the new adventure with his sister and brother they had planned after his return from the Octopus Islands. As he swam out to Octavia's den, he could feel the warm sun on his back and sense the slight rise in water temperature. He could see the first of the summer kayakers on the beach in the Bretons and thought about a short detour ashore to raid a lunchbox or two. However, the lure of adventure pulled even stronger than his desire for food or mischief, and he continued directly to Octavia's.

He found his sister already tidying up her den in preparation for leaving and gave her a hand so they could leave for Omar's right away. They decided to meet Omar, have some lunch, and then head south toward Gorge Harbor on Cortes Island. Oscar had fond memories of his time there with Omar and wanted to share the place with Octavia as well.

They arrived at Omar's den to find that he, too, was of the same mind and had already made himself ready to go. They dove for a quick lunch of fish and oysters and then set off along the shore to Cortes Island. They watched the little ferry to Heriot Bay leave Whaletown and decided to pop into the harbor to see if there was any excitement to be had. The marina was quiet, however, and did not present any opportunities for mischief.

They swam on to the channel between Cortes and Marina and found the tide to be running out of Gorge Harbor at a rather furious pace so they went ashore on Marina Island and gathered a few clams in the shallows for a snack while waiting for slack tide.

The tide stopped running just as the sun was setting, so the three siblings paddled through the narrow opening in the rocks into Gorge Harbor. Oscar and Omar were anxious to see what mischief they could get into, but Octavia was struck by the beauty of the harbor in the wonderful twilight and insisted that they do some exploring before launching into their normal otter pranks.

They did a quick tour of the harbor, ending up in the marina just as night was falling. The people on the boats were moving inside, and lights started to come on in the boats and on the docks. The otters checked out the swim platforms of the boats and found several with containers that they decided to explore after the lights went out. They did not have too long to wait and were soon on the platform of a huge yacht that had a large open tank on it. Inside, they found quite a haul of fresh crabs and began to devour them with great gusto. Unfortunately, in their enthusiasm, they created quite a racket, which aroused the people on the boat. The three otters splashed into the water just a moment before the door to the swim platform opened, and a man with a large broom appeared. He had certainly intended to use the broom on whoever—or whatever—was on his boat, but seeing no one, he did find it handy for cleaning up the rather large mess the three had left.

With this wonderful experience launching their adventure, they swam to one of the little islands in the harbor and found a safe and warm place to settle in for the night.

Chapter two
More Fun on Cortes

With the coming of daylight, the three siblings explored the rest of their little island and then swam over to another slightly larger one. There were several houses on this island, but people were starting to move around and come outside, so the three took off to the resort that Oscar and Omar had found on their last visit. There was a float moored off shore that children staying at the resort used as a base for swimming and diving. No one was there when they arrived, so all of them hopped up on the platform and began showing off by scurrying all over, playing a game of tag, which always ended with one of them falling in the water with a giant splash.

This attracted the attention of some children who were playing on the shore, and in no time, they were swimming out to look at the otters. The three of them spent over an hour showing off their aquatic tricks for the children, who laughed and clapped their hands at every feat. Finally a large dog that had been on the shore decided to swim out to the float so the otters did one last series of spectacular twists and dives and left before the dog arrived.

With all of this fun, they found that they had worked up quite an appetite, and Oscar and Omar knew just how to take care of that. They showed Octavia the floats where people were farming the mussels and oysters. They dove down along the strands on which the shellfish grew and helped themselves to quite a meal.

The otters spent the rest of the day exploring all of the rest of Gorge Harbor and were quite taken by the beauty of it. While they were taking a break from their explorations, they made plans for the next part of their travels. Their father had told Oscar of other harbors and inlets on Cortes that were just as interesting and beautiful so they decided right then to take them all in. The next one would be Cortes Bay, but Oscar recalled that Father had told him it was a rather long swim from Gorge. In preparation, they would make it an early night, planning to set off with the morning's outgoing tide.

This settled, they found a snug little cove with some nice soft moss to make into a bed, grabbed a few more mussels and oysters from the floats, and curled up for a good night's sleep.

Chapter three
The Next Bay

Dawn arrived early, but Oscar, Omar, and Octavia were ready to go. The outgoing tide swept them through the narrow opening of the harbor and into the channel between Marina and Cortes Islands. It was quite a long swim along Cortes, and they did not take time to explore several other coves along the way but did stop to forage for some shellfish in the shoals close to the shore. They finally rounded the southern tip of Cortes and continued up along the shore, passing two small islands on their way. Evening was again approaching when they rounded a small point of land and spotted a good-size bay with docks and many boats. They were very tired from their long swim so chose to put off exploration till they were fully rested.

The next morning was gray and rainy, which did not make any difference to the three otters, but the people on the boats stayed in their cabins, for the most part. This did give the travelers an opportunity to check out their surroundings without interference from people or dogs. Once in a while, they would venture onto a swim platform to see what they could find, but there was not much to get into. They did rouse a few dogs, however, and had a grand time setting them off into fits of barking that broke the peace and quiet of the bay.

They stayed in Cortes Bay another day, but when the sun came out the next day, they voted to move on up the coast. The shoreline just out of Cortes Bay was quite interesting, with many inlets and coves, and the three of them ducked into all of them, finding good food and warm places to sleep. After they rounded another point, they had a good view quite a ways up the shore of the island and could not see much of interest.

Oscar remembered their father had told of another bay called Squirrel Cove that was supposed to offer some very special treats, so they decided to keep going until they found it. During their rather long swim, they noticed a number of boats going into what had to be an inlet, so they picked up their pace until they came to a wide opening into a large bay. They could see lots of boats, a dock, and a small village along one shore, and Oscar knew this had to be the Squirrel Cove of his father's tales.

Chapter four
Something Different

Being tired from their strenuous swim, the three otters rested on an island at the mouth of the harbor and surveyed the scene. There were many boats at anchor in the cove and lots of adults, children, and dogs coming and going in dinghies. There was so much activity they could barely take it all in. They knew this would be an extended stay.

The first order of business was to get a feel for the entire area, so they opted for a leisurely paddle around the shore of the cove without trying to attract a lot of attention. As they passed by a group of logs rafted together, they noticed a house had been built on the raft. As they came closer, a wonderful aroma came to their nostrils. Omar and Octavia had never smelled anything so delicious, but Oscar recognized it immediately from the big room at the inn near his den on Quadra. He told his brother and sister that they HAD to return to this place.

As they pressed on into the cove, they saw much activity at one end. Swimming carefully nearer, they could see people using little inflatable boats and inner tubes to run a small rapids. This looked like a lot of fun, so they held back until there were no people present and then made a beeline for the narrow opening. They were immediately swept through, grazing some of the smooth rocks on the bottom, and into another bay, which had a small island in the middle. The ride was very fast and fun, so they scrambled to the shore and made their way back to the opening. Again waiting until no people were around, they jumped into the water and were swept through again. Octavia started giggling and swallowed so much water that the boys had to pull her to shore and let her cough it up. They all had a good laugh and knew this was going to be a frequent place to visit during their stay in Squirrel Cove.

"Octavia started giggling and swallowed so much water ..."

When Octavia had recovered, they resumed their swim around the cove and came to a large tidal flat, which was far too shallow for a boat moorage and had such a soft bottom that people and dogs did not venture into it. This was the perfect place for a rest stop and became even more perfect when they found the bottom covered with large clams. They feasted on the shellfish and found a place on shore to spend the night. As they settled in, Oscar had a strange feeling they were being watched, but he let it go and fell asleep.

Chapter five
A New Friend

When Oscar awoke, he found his siblings still sleeping. The weird feeling of being watched still hung over him so he got up quietly and scanned the surrounding area. He could not see anything but heard a slight rustling in some bushes off to one side. He pretended to ignore the area but noticed a tiny motion in the underbrush. Still not making any sign that he sensed anything out of the ordinary, he casually wandered in the general direction until he felt he was close enough and then plunged into the bushes—hopefully prepared for whatever he might find. He got a glimpse of a small brownish shape and pounced on it. After some squealing and a bit of a struggle, the shape went still and quiet.

Oscar looked down at the creature in his grasp and found, much to his surprise, another otter. Smaller than Oscar, it had much more dainty features, more like his sister, Octavia. When the other otter recovered from being pounced on, Oscar immediately let it up and introduced himself. The other otter looked at him with the cutest eyes he had ever seen and introduced HERself as Daphne.

Oscar found himself at a loss for words for probably the first time in his rather short life. He stammered out something about his brother and sister and pointed in the general direction of where he had left them and motioned for Daphne to follow him.

They found Omar and Octavia just waking up, yawning and stretching, and Oscar hastened to introduce his new friend. They spent quite some time in conversation about where they were each from and how they had come to be in Squirrel Cove. It turned out that Daphne had a den in another large cove known as Von Donop Inlet, which was across Cortes Island from where they were now.

She explained that a trail through the woods from the tide flats led to her inlet and she would be happy to show them the way if they would like to explore it. Oscar said he had heard about the trail from his father and would be delighted to explore it. Omar said he had noticed the mouth of an inlet on one of his swims north from his den on Read Island but he had not taken the time to enter and investigate. The three siblings readily agreed to take Daphne up on her offer—after they had thoroughly checked out all that Squirrel Cove had to offer.

Daphne said she had come over to the cove a number of times but this was the first time she had ever encountered other otters. Since she had not had the benefit of company, her explorations of the cove had been very limited. They all decided to make their investigation of the area a team effort and started to lay out a plan. Daphne was excited about running the rapids into the lagoon, so they elected to make that the first joint adventure.

As they had been chatting for quite a while, they discovered they were very hungry. At this point, something popped into Oscar's mind as he remembered that wonderful smell they had encountered when they had first come into the cove. He suggested that they make the house on the log raft their first stop before going to the rapids. They all heartily agreed and set forth immediately across the cove.

Chapter six
A Sweet Treat

When they arrived at the log raft, they saw many dinghies tied up to it with people going into the house and coming out with trays of buns. The smell of these buns really amplified their hunger, and Omar, Octavia, and Daphne all looked at Oscar as if to say, "What now?"

During the swim over, Oscar had worked out a plan, which he now shared with them: they would leave Octavia and Daphne hiding in cracks in the logs near one of the dinghies while the two boys would sneak up close to the house and follow the people as they emerged with the trays of goodies.

Soon they were rewarded when a large lady came out of the house with a very large tray and headed toward the dinghy where the girls were hiding. Just before the lady got to her boat, Oscar motioned to Daphne and Octavia to get ready, and he and Omar made themselves obvious to the lady and ran right between her legs. Extremely startled, she let out a scream, threw her arms up in the air, and let go of the trays, which went flying. All four otters made a beeline for a bun, grabbed it, and ran to shore on the logs. Oscar made sure they kept their treasures dry, remembering how he had ruined a loaf of bread he had grabbed with his two raccoon buddies.

They hurried into some woods and lay down completely out of breath and laughing hysterically, but holding on tightly to their sweet-smelling buns. It turned out that the buns tasted even better than they smelled, and they each savored the treat and started planning when they would make their next attempt.

Oscar remembered from his adventure with the raccoons that people tended to learn from their mistakes and change they way they did things so as to make it harder for the mischief-makers. He told the others they should probably wait a few days before another raid since there would be a whole new bunch of boaters in the cove that would not be aware of their ruse. With this good advice in mind, they all set off to have some fun in the rapids and did so for the next few hours.

"Extremely startled she let out a scream, threw her arms up in the air, ..."

Chapter seven
Summer Fun

The four otters spent the better part of the next month playing in Squirrel Cove. They never seemed to tire of running the little rapids into the lagoon and swimming out to the tiny island in the middle. They explored the island and the shoreline around the lagoon and made many friends of the creatures they encountered in the woods.

They made raids on the customers of the bakery house on the log raft about twice a week and had a few close calls but never failed in getting away with some savory treats. As a matter of fact, the baker who lived in the house became quite fond of them and once even put out a whole tray of the buns just for the otters. Oscar figured that he did it so they would not take them from his customers, so they left him alone for a few extra days to show their appreciation.

This did not stop them from their raids on the boaters' swim platforms at night or their upsetting dogs at every opportunity. With four of them at work, they kept the cove hopping most of the time. The children on the boats were fun to amuse with various otter antics, and each one of them found their own special way to show off for the audience.

One of their favorite games was to wait until they spotted a dinghy with some children and a dog in it and then swim up under water and all pop out right next to the boat at the same time. This would drive the dog absolutely crazy, make the children howl with laughter, and entertain the otters immensely. They finally decided to quit this game after one day when a very large dog almost capsized the small dinghy and one young boy was thrown overboard. Fortunately, he had on a life vest, and the children were able to get him back in the boat without mishap, but they were obviously quite frightened, and the otters sensed that perhaps some of the fun had gone out of the game.

Finally, one morning, Daphne told the others that she needed to get back to check on her den in Von Donop Inlet, and she invited them all to come with her. They all readily agreed so she led them to the tide flats where they had met and showed them the trail leading off through the woods.

"The children were able to get him back in the boat
without mishap ..."

Chapter eight
New Places

The trail led them through a beautiful forest and rose for a ways before descending gently along a small stream. The stillness in the woods was broken only by the babbling of the stream and the occasional call of an unseen raven. The light was also quite soft due to the large trees and the underbrush so they all blinked when the trail ended on a bright sunny beach.

The three siblings were all very taken with the beauty and complimented Daphne on the location for her den. Oscar was especially impressed and went on and on about the place. Daphne was a little embarrassed by his extensive praise, and Octavia nudged Omar and gave him a little wink. Omar nudged her back. They could both tell that Oscar was enamored more by Daphne than by the location, but they said nothing and just let him ramble until he seemed to run out of words.

Daphne showed them inside her den, which was absolutely lovely, and she offered to let them all stay with her. It was a bit crowded, but none of them seemed to mind, especially Oscar. After they had foraged dinner, Daphne showed them her end of the inlet. They swam all around and noticed there were very few boats here, compared to all of the activity in Squirrel Cove. However, they were all so impressed by the natural beauty that they enjoyed the relative peace and quiet.

They were all beginning to feel tired after their walk through the forest and their extended swim, so they returned to Daphne's den and snuggled in for the night. Daphne promised to show them the rest of the inlet the next morning, and they were all soon fast asleep.

The next day, they covered another arm of the inlet and then proceeded out toward the mouth. Daphne showed them a rather large stream tumbling down over some rocks, which were also strewn with logs and bushes. She told them that there was a lake from which the stream originated, and they all decided to explore it right away.

The lake was even prettier than the rest of the inlet and completely devoid of people. The stream was too shallow for even very small boats, so any visitors had to make it up the streambed, which was a difficult climb. There was a large island in the lake, which they decided to make the base camp for their explorations. Daphne told them there was a lot to see around the lake and island, so they decided to spend several days there.

They first found a snug temporary den that would accommodate all four of them and gathered some moss to make it more comfortable. Then the four set out to see what the lake had to offer. One of their first finds was a bed of freshwater clams, which they tried immediately. They all determined that they were not as tasty as the salt-water variety but were so large that a couple were a complete meal. They also found small fish in the lake, which were a new and quite acceptable supplement to their diet.

The woods around the lake were teeming with other small wildlife, and they were able to make some new friends who showed them other sights and shared food tips. Daphne remembered that there were two beavers that had a home on the island, so they swam out for a visit. The beavers were quite friendly and welcomed them but were so busy running around doing things that they never took time to sit down and chat. Finally, the otters determined it was time to leave, but the beavers only stopped from their work long enough to wave goodbye and then returned to their labors. The otters could never actually figure out just what the beavers were doing, but they certainly were busy.

After several days, Octavia and Omar announced that they felt it was about time to head back to their own dens since they had been away for nearly two months. Oscar, however, said he would like to stay on a bit, and Daphne seemed quite pleased with this, so the siblings parted company and left the other two to themselves.

Chapter nine
New Feelings

scar and Daphne made their way back to her den and spent the next couple of weeks sharing new experiences and getting to know each other better. They found they had much in common, but Oscar definitely had more of the adventurer in him, obviously inherited from his father, while Daphne liked the security of her own surroundings.

This did not, however, diminish the growing feeling of affection each had for the other. This was something new for each of them, and they were a bit unsure of just what to do with it. They would play and laugh together during the day and snuggle at night in Daphne's warm den, where they would tell stories and giggle until they fell asleep.

Oscar knew that he wanted to spend most of his time with Daphne, but the call of adventure was very strong within him. Finally, one day, he told her that he needed to go check out his own den and asked if she would come with him for at least a visit. Daphne was a bit reluctant since she had never been off Cortes Island but at last agreed to go with him for a few days.

They swam out of Von Donop Inlet and found themselves just across the channel from Read Island so decided to stop in to see Omar on their way to Oscar's. They spent a brief time with Omar and then went by Octavia's as well. It was getting dark by the time they rounded to the little islet in front of Oscar's den. They paused only for a short meal of clams and oysters before settling in for the night.

Daphne was very impressed with they way Oscar had set up his den and at how large it was. This made Oscar feel quite proud, and he was happy that Daphne seemed right at home. He told her he would introduce her to some of his friends in the morning, and they fell quickly to sleep.

Chapter ten
Some Important News

The morning brought brilliant sunshine and an extremely low tide. They emerged from the den, and Oscar showed Daphne down to the beach on the islet, where his friends the minks were already scurrying about on the rocks. They welcomed Daphne warmly and were soon joined by the young deer, now beginning to grow quite large and truly dwarfing his companions. They were just settling in to a get-acquainted brunch when the two raccoon brothers came out of the woods and, in an extremely excited fashion, ran across the flats to the beach and began chattering away, both at the same time. They were so excited that it took several minutes before one of them ran out of breath and the group could begin to piece together the story.

Evidently, they were wandering through the woods nearby when they heard a sort of whimper, then a howl, and then the whimper again. They cautiously crept towards where they heard the sounds and peeked out into a small clearing, in the middle of which was a large wolf with one hind leg caught in a snare. The wolf was in a great deal of pain but was able to ask the raccoons for help. They were understandably wary of this large predator, but he assured them he would do them no harm.

When they got nearer, they could see that the snare wire had dug deeply into the wolf's leg, and it was bleeding. They tried to loosen the wire, but their claws were just too large to undo it so they ran to the beach to see if their friends were there.

The raccoons asked if Oscar or the minks might be able to help. The minks respectfully declined, not wanting to put themselves anywhere near a wolf. As was to be expected, the deer had no intention of helping, either, and had the perfect excuse that his hooves would be of little use.

Oscar could not think of an excuse to refuse help. Besides, Daphne's presence made everything a little different, somehow. Oscar told Daphne to wait with the minks and deer while he accompanied the raccoons back to the clearing. Daphne was very concerned for Oscar's safety, but he put on a brave face, told her not to worry, and set off with the brothers.

"The wolf was practically unconscious with the pain ..."

When they came to the clearing, they could see that the wolf was practically unconscious with the pain, but he was able to understand that Oscar would try to help him, and he assured the otter that he would be safe. Oscar set to work as gently as he could with his sharp teeth and small claws and finally slightly loosened the wire holding the wolf's leg. With this little bit of slack, one of the raccoons was able to get a claw in, and between the two of them, they opened the snare enough to slip it off the wolf's leg.

All four animals fell back in complete exhaustion from the tension and took a few minutes to gather their thoughts. Oscar pointed out that whoever had set the snare would certainly come back soon to check it out and they must all be as far away as possible, especially the wolf. The wolf could not have agreed more, and the raccoons assisted the wolf up on his three good legs. He was able to take a few steps and told them that he thought he could make his way to his own den. Oscar and the raccoons said they would cover his trail as best they could.

The wolf thanked the three profusely and promised to remember them and to tell all the other wolves not to harm them. With that, he limped off, and the three friends did what they could to disguise the wolf's trail so that whoever set the snare would not be able to easily follow him. They then rushed back to the beach to tell their other friends of their harrowing experience.

When they got to the beach, the others ran to meet them and were relieved that they had returned safely. Daphne was VERY impressed with Oscar's bravery, which made him VERY proud. They were also cheered by the promise that the wolf made to tell the other wolves to protect the animals that had saved him. All in all, it was quite an adventure, and they all slept very soundly that night.

Chapter eleven
The Parting

Daphne stayed with Oscar for several weeks. They had great fun with all of the other animals, had gigantic feasts of seafood, and played on the rock slide that Oscar's mother had taken him to when he was very young. The inn was also in operation, and the Oscar-dog made frequent appearances, so they had fun teasing him whenever they got the chance. They made a couple of trips up to the big deck with the room full of wonderful smells. There were too many people around for them to get inside, but they did enjoy playing games with children who came to the inn and went out on the dinghy or kayaks.

One day, when the weather had cooled and the sun was rising later and setting earlier, Daphne announced she should get back to her den to make sure it was all right. Oscar really did not want her to leave, but she was determined to head home, so he prevailed upon her at least to allow him to accompany her on her journey. This made him feel a bit better, but he knew it was not going to be as much fun when she left.

They had a grand party with all of the animals on the little beach before she left, and Daphne knew she had made some very good friends whose company she enjoyed immensely and she would visit frequently.

She gave a big hug to the raccoons and minks, and the deer bent down so she could hug his neck. He decided to give her a lick of affection but only succeeded in giving her a good soaking, which made all of them laugh.

The two otters set out the next morning, stopping by the Bretons to check in with Octavia and then going by Omar's as well. They did not make it to Daphne's den until almost nightfall, so they gathered a small meal of shellfish and settled in for the night. Oscar did not sleep all that well. He was not looking forward to returning to his own den … or, at least, returning without Daphne.

He did stay for a few days but finally realized that both he and Daphne needed to put their dens in order for the winter. Then it occurred to him that his father might be making a visit in the near future, and he had something to look forward to at home since this time HE had a few tales of his own to tell. With this in mind, he said goodbye to Daphne and set off for home.

Chapter twelve
Catch-up Time

J ust because he had not been there for a while, Oscar decided to go home via Whiterock Passage, which he had traversed coming home from his first big adventure with his father. The passage was just as beautiful as when he had first seen it. The shallow water over the round rocks and the sea grass growing up from the bottom made it all so peaceful that he got a warm feeling of comfort that helped relieve the pain of leaving Daphne. In fact, he decided to make a point of bringing Daphne here when they next got together.

He arrived home and set about making his den extra special in anticipation of his father's coming. As it turned out, Oscar had had the right feeling because Father appeared at his door within two weeks. They had a joyful reunion, and Oscar was proud to show his father how he had fixed up the den. When Father had expressed his pleasure at his son's handiwork, Oscar proudly revealed the secret passage to the rear of his den he had found and concealed. Father was even more impressed and told his son to keep it to himself since he never knew when he might need it, and the fewer that were aware, the better.

Respectfully, Oscar asked Father to fill him in on his travels of the last year and listened attentively to the stories. However, Father admitted that he was slowing down a bit and not quite up to the long distances he had covered in the past. Oscar was surprised at this since his father seemed always to be on the go and ready for a new experience or adventure. Father explained that he still had all of the old feelings but he thought he would keep a little closer to his children and perhaps see a bit more of them. Oscar told Father of the two new kits Mother had, and this made his decision even firmer.

When Father had finished with his tales, it was Oscar's turn. He told his father that he did not want to tell everything since Omar and Octavia had shared most of his experiences, and they would like to tell their own versions of what had happened. So, he just gave Father the outline of the trip around Cortes, but he HAD to tell about meeting Daphne. Father seemed very pleased at this news and gave Oscar a big hug.

Then, Oscar told of his adventure with the wolf. For the first time ever, his father seemed at a loss for words. He actually made Oscar repeat the whole story several times, just to make sure he got all of the details. He said he was so proud of his son for several reasons. First, he had shown great bravery in approaching such a dangerous creature, and second, he had shown wonderful compassion in helping another animal in distress. Father said he had had very little contact with wolves, but he had found them to be true to their word, and Oscar had made a valuable ally that he might come to need at some point.

They spent the rest of the night just chatting about other possible adventures and looking forward to being in more frequent contact in the future. At last, they fell fast asleep and did not awaken until mid-morning. Father said he would visit Mother and the new kits and then get together with Octavia and Omar before coming back to Oscar's.

The reunion had gone VERY well, and Oscar knew that he had pleased his father, which made him happy. He also felt he was growing up, and he did not know exactly what to make of it. He knew he still loved fun and games and getting into mischief, but he also knew some things had changed and there was such a thing as responsibility—something he had never given a thought to before.

With these new ideas swirling around in his head, he decided to discuss them with Father and his siblings when they got together, and now he could hardly wait for them all to come back.

WHERE DO WE GO FROM HERE?

BOOK FIVE

A New Family Begins

Chapter one
A Family Reunion

Father Otter had returned to the area and, after his wonderful time with Oscar, had set out to visit Mother, Omar, and Octavia, promising to return to Oscar's before he left on another adventure.

Oscar had been really looking forward to his father's return and was thrilled when he heard outside his den one morning the sounds of his entire family. His father had told the others of Oscar's brave deed with the wolf, and they all wanted to congratulate him and hear the story for themselves.

Omar and Octavia were very impressed with their little brother and told him so. His mother was also extremely proud, and the two new kits, which came along with Mother, were absolutely in awe. Mother was also very interested in hearing more about Daphne, and Oscar was more than happy to oblige.

Oscar had to tell the wolf story at least three times, but he tried to be a little modest in letting everyone know that the raccoon brothers had been a part of the adventure and had been the ones who had initially found the wolf in the woods. As it turned out, the raccoon brothers were coming down for lunch at the little beach and stopped in to see if

Oscar wanted to join them. Oscar was quick to accept and to introduce the raccoons to his entire family.

The whole troop marched off to the beach and were soon joined by the deer and the minks. They had a grand time and a giant feast, and all shared stories and played games. The two new kits joined in the fun and were immediately adopted by Oscar's friends, who insisted that Mother bring them by even if Oscar was not there so they could play together.

What with all the tales and games, along with the eating, the lunch ran on well into the late afternoon. Mother finally said it was time for her to get the new little ones off to their den, and the other animals decided to get back to their normal routines. Father, Omar, and Octavia, however, stayed on with Oscar and made plans to spend the night in his now-large den and talk about the future.

The four of them retired to Oscar's den and made themselves comfortable. The three siblings wanted to know what adventures Father had planned and gathered around him with rapt attention. Father repeated what he had told Oscar earlier—that he was slowing down a bit and wanted to stay a little closer to his family. He did say, however, he felt he had one more big trip in him. He had heard about a fairly large city to the south, which he said he would like to see before he retired. The city was called Nanaimo, and there was a large and active harbor with much bigger ferries than those on Quadra, and also ocean-going cargo ships.

Oscar and his siblings were amazed by what their father described and told him they could not wait for his return to get all of the details. Oscar expressed some interest in seeing the city himself, but the other two thought that they would content themselves with hearing about it from Father. Then Father asked Oscar if he would like to accompany him on this journey. Oscar was truly flattered that his father would want him on such a major trip but said he would have to sleep on it.

They all agreed that a little sleep was a good idea and so settled in for the night.

Chapter two
The Decision

Oscar did not sleep very well that night; too many things were turning over in his head. He had a strong desire to take off on any new adventure, but he also had a strange feeling, which he could not quite place, that he had something he needed to stay around for. Then it finally hit him: DAPHNE! He felt relieved he had identified the feeling, but now he did not know what to do about it. He tossed and turned. At last, he decided to talk to Father and his brother and sister in the morning, and he was able to drop off to sleep.

When they all awoke, Oscar knew what he needed to do. He announced he would accompany Father on the long journey to the south but he had to do something first. Omar looked at Octavia and winked, and she smiled. They both asked if it had anything to do with Daphne, but before they could make fun of Oscar's reply, Father said of course Oscar would need to consult Daphne and he would be honored to go along with Oscar to explain to her the hazards.

Oscar felt a great respect for Father, not just because he had prevented a potential embarrassing moment with his siblings but also because he understood what was going through Oscar's mind. Father then went on to explain he and Oscar would have to spend some time making plans for their departure, but they would check in with Daphne first.

After breakfast, the four set out for Octavia's den and dropped her off. Continuing on to Omar's, Father and Oscar parted from Omar and then proceeded up to Daphne's inlet, which Father said he had not visited for many years but recalled because of its natural beauty. They made their way down the inlet to Daphne's den and found her at home.

She was pleased to meet Oscar's father and told him she had heard many tales of his adventures from Oscar. They gathered shellfish for a meal, and Daphne noticed Oscar was not his usual bubbly self. She finally asked if something was on his mind and could see he was having a tough time coming up with words, which was VERY unusual.

Again, Father came to Oscar's rescue. He started by telling Daphne that he was going to be making a journey, which might be his last big trip, and he had asked his son to join him. He explained there might be some danger involved but it would be lessened if there were two of them—an extra pair of eyes and ears, as Father put it. He described the route they would take, explained it would take several months to get there and back, and told what sights they were expecting to see. He then asked if Daphne had any questions or concerns.

She told them she would like to think about what was involved before making any comments, and Father agreed that was the right approach. He then said he would leave the two of them to discuss the matter and return to Oscar's den to make his own plans for departure.

After Father left, neither of them said anything for a long time. Finally, Daphne moved close to Oscar and gave him a big hug. She said she could tell he really wanted to go and she would not stop him, but she did ask if he would stay with her for a day or two before he left. Oscar agreed at once, and they snuggled in for the night.

Chapter three
A Tearful Farewell

The morning dawned clear and cold. Daphne and Oscar could see their breath as they peeked out the entrance to Daphne's den. It was so beautiful that Oscar had a brief moment of regret in leaving both this gorgeous inlet and Daphne for a number of months. Daphne did not make it any easier since she came close to him and gave him a hug.

They dove for fish and shared a quiet meal on the beach. No other creatures were around, except for the birds that seemed to echo Oscar's sorrow in their mournful calls. The two otters wandered through the woods for a bit and tried to play their usual games, but neither of them enjoyed them very much as their thoughts always seemed to come around to their impending separation.

Oscar spent three days with Daphne before he decided that he needed to rejoin his father to make plans. He knew if he stayed much longer, he might not leave, and after all, he HAD made the decision to go. He gave Daphne a long nuzzle and then slipped into the water for the lonely swim back to his own den.

When he returned to his den, he found his father and two siblings, who had come over to bid the travelers a safe journey. Omar and Octavia also wanted to see if Oscar would actually go through with it and were fully prepared to give him a bad time if he backed out. This, however, firmed up his resolution.

Oscar made his den all tidy and buttoned it up for the winter and then made the rounds of his friends to say goodbye. The minks expressed grave concern about the otters' safety, but the raccoon brothers were excited about the prospects for new ideas for tricks and mischief that Oscar might pick up in his travels. The deer, even though he was now fairly well grown, being the relatively timid creature that he was, just looked concerned and sad.

Father assured all of Oscar's friends they would be careful and watch out for each other and return safely in the spring. They all shared one more feast on the little beach, and then Father and Oscar retired to rest up for the long trip.

The next morning, when Father and Oscar emerged from the den to depart, all of Oscar's friends had gathered on the beach to wave to them and shout encouragement, even though there were a few tears mixed in.

Chapter four
Rounding the Point

As Father and Oscar paddled south toward Heriot Bay, Mother and the new kits were out in front of their den waving. The two did not stop. Oscar could see that even his father had had enough farewells so they just waved back and swam on by. As they paddled on, Father told Oscar the plan was to round the south end of Quadra Island, Cape Mudge, cross over to Campbell River on Vancouver Island, and see if they could pick up a lift on a boat or a barge headed south.

There was not a lot of traffic in the winter, and many of the vessels were just too large for them to get onto, so Father said it might take some time to find the right lift. It took them the better part of the day to make it to the cape, and when they got there, the tide was running through the passage at such a pace that they had to wait for slack to cross the channel between the islands.

They settled in to some logs on the beach and listened to the thundering roar of the currents rushing by in the channel. As it began to get dark, the sound of the water diminished and at last became very still. In the lights of the small city of Campbell River on Vancouver Island, they could see barely a ripple on the surface of the water, and Father indicated it was time to make the crossing. Oscar thought it was a little scary swimming in the dark, and he could hear the engine of what must have been a very large craft moving through the channel.

Father and son kept a wary eye out for any lights on the boat and finally saw the running lights of a slow-moving tugboat towing an enormous barge that loomed as a huge black shape on the surface far behind. Farther told Oscar the barge would be a great ride but it was far too high for them to climb aboard from the water. He said if they located one at a dock in a marina in town they might be able to find a way to get on.

They saw the little ferry coming across the channel from Quadra Island and then spotted the lights marking the entrance to the channel into the ferry slip. They followed the ferry into the small harbor and swam into the marina that was next to the ferry dock. In the dark, they could not tell if any of the boats were occupied, so they found a place under a float and waited till daylight.

In the morning, they could see that all of the boats in the marina were sealed up for the winter so Father said they would have to check out some other marinas if they wanted to find a ride south. They swam along close to the shore, which was a rock jetty, so they did not get out into the current in the large channel. They entered a second marina but found the same situation with the boats there.

On their third stop, there were more commercial vessels, and it appeared that one of them was preparing to depart south for the rest of the winter. There was a gangplank down to the float where the boat was moored, so they took cover and waited until they were sure no one was coming and then scampered aboard. On the aft deck, there were crab traps piled high and a lifeboat with a canvas cover, which they decided would be a perfect place to hide for their trip.

They had no sooner hidden themselves beneath the cover than they heard the crew come aboard and begin to prepare to sail. Soon the gangplank was hauled up, and the engines were started. Lines were cast off, and the boat pulled slowly out of the marina and into the channel. The otters took a peek out to make sure the boat turned south, and then they settled in to figure out how to pilfer dinner.

Chapter five
Things That Go Bump in the Night

The boat did not proceed far down the channel before pulling into another marina and up to another dock. As the otters peered out from their hiding place, they could see men bringing a hose from the dock up onto the deck. They took the cap off a pipe coming through the deck and inserted the hose into the opening. Oscar's nostrils picked up a strong and unpleasant odor, and Father explained that it was from the diesel fuel being pumped into the tanks of the boat.

It took quite a while to fill up the tanks, and it was almost dark when they finished the fueling and pulled away from the dock. The crew all went inside the cabin, and the cook started making preparations for dinner. Oscar and Father watched intently to figure out when to make their move. They could see the cook put out a number of large slabs of salmon and knew that it would be a special meal tonight.

The crew was in a forward salon and was making a lot of noise. The cook would go in periodically with an armload of bottles and then come back to the galley a few minutes later. Every time he came back, the otters watched as he threw his head back and drained one of these bottles. The crew was getting noisier all of the time, and Father said they would make a dash for the galley the next time the cook left.

They did not have to wait long, and as soon as the cook left, the otters were out of the lifeboat and into the galley. Father grabbed a good-sized hunk of fresh salmon while Oscar picked up as many eggs as he could carry from a bowl on a counter. They were back, well under cover, before the cook returned, drained another bottle, and started to put the salmon on the grill. He did not seem to notice that one slab of fish was missing.

The two otters shared a wonderful meal of salmon and eggs, and although they were both quite full, they decided to see if they might snag another little treat for later. When they lifted the cover on the lifeboat, they saw that the boat had entered a dense fog bank. They could barely see across the deck to the door to the galley.

Just as they were climbing out of their hiding place, a loud screeching noise came from below. The boat rocked violently from side to side and came to an abrupt stop, throwing them out of the lifeboat, onto the deck, across it, and into the side of the cabin. Both were dazed for a moment or two and tried to figure out what had happened. The boat was now listing at a rather sharp angle, and they could hear frantic shouts from the crew and the sound of various alarms.

Father told Oscar that the boat must have run aground and might well be sinking. He led Oscar to a place on the deck where it was closest to the water and told him to jump. The two of them hit the water at the same time, and even though they had jumped from the lowest part of the deck, it was still a rather long drop to the surface. When they hit the water, they realized that it was quite shallow and the bottom was very rocky.

They watched as all of the deck lights came on, and the crew struggled across the steeply tilting deck to the lifeboat and attempted to lower it. After what seemed like a very long time, the crew finally got the lifeboat into the water and ladders down to it, and men began getting board. The main boat was apparently hard aground and not in immediate danger of sinking, but that was certainly not obvious from the violent nature of the impact.

Oscar and his father did not mind being in the cold water, of course, but the crew did not share the animals' tolerance for icy cold surroundings and was happy to be in the lifeboat. Soon, the otters decided they had had enough of it, too, and made for shore with Father leading the way. They found a beach with some rocks and bushes, although they could not see much in the fog. There was also some driftwood, and they fashioned a rude windbreak out of it and curled up for some well-earned sleep feeling they were two very lucky otters.

"Throwing them out of the lifeboat, onto the deck, across it ..."

Chapter six
Exploring the Coast

When the otters awoke the next morning, the fog still lay in a blanket across the water. They could just make out the dark outline of the crab boat sitting high and dry on the rocks. The tide had gone out, and the boat looked ridiculous perched up in the air like a bird too big for its nest. There was no sign of the lifeboat and the crew. Father said another boat probably had picked them up or they had gone ashore somewhere along this stretch of coastline.

The father and son stretched and discovered they had more than a few sore spots from their tumble across the deck, but their injuries did not appear to be serious. Oscar asked if Father had any idea where they were, but he did not get a specific response. Instead, the elder otter simply motioned to the water, and the two started swimming slowly in the direction they felt was south.

Due to their sore bodies, they had to stop frequently to rest, and it was a few hours before they spotted what appeared to be a large white mountain visible through the fog. As they neared it, they saw it was a beach and giant mound of oyster shells. These had obviously come from a commercial operation in the vicinity, although they could not see any buildings in the fog. They came ashore and climbed up the oyster mountain for a better view. The fog was still too thick for them to see very far, even from the top of the mound, but Father said he could just make out the shape of what might be a building not far away.

They approached cautiously and found the oyster processing plant, which was in operation. They could hear people moving about and the sounds of machinery. They also spotted a number of bins of harvested oysters waiting to be brought into the plant. Never wanting to pass up a free meal, they grabbed a few and retreated to the mound to enjoy their catch.

Both otters were still sore and very tired from their swim, so they decided to find shelter and rest until the fog cleared and they could see a bit more of the surroundings. They moved on down the shore a bit and came to what looked like another boat up on the beach. As they went ashore, they could see that this boat was put there on purpose and looked as if it might have been a café at some point.

They walked up the gangplank to the main deck and saw the doors and windows were boarded up. As they went around the deck, they found a board over one of the windows was hanging from a rusty nail. With almost no effort, they were able to pull the board off and gain access to the inside of the old boat. The place had not been used in quite some time and smelled a bit musty, but it was definitely warmer than the damp, foggy outdoors and was dry. They found some old towels and pillows and arranged them into comfortable beds and collapsed for a long sleep.

When they finally stirred, it was dark outside, but they went out to look over the immediate area. The fog was still there but seemed a little less thick. No houses or people were nearby, and they had a warm den with an unlimited supply of harvested oysters, so father and son agreed that this was a perfect place to spend a little time. That decision made, they returned to the boat and settled in for a stay.

Chapter seven
On Southward

The father-and-son team stayed in the old boat for about a week. When the fog cleared, they could see they were on a lovely bay, which they had pretty much to themselves. The oyster processing plant was quite small, so there were not a lot of people around, which allowed the otters to help themselves to fresh seafood whenever they wished.

When their bruises from the shipwreck healed, Father announced they should be on their way. He figured they had covered only about half of the distance to the city when their free ride had ended. Before they left, they put the board back over the window so they might have a private place to stay on their way home.

The journey south was uneventful. They did meet some other otters and had a good time swapping stories. Their new friends had not ventured to the city and thus could not give them any tips, but they did wish them well and asked that they stop in on their way back and fill them in on the experience.

As they proceeded along the coast, they saw more signs of people and even a few small cities. At one point, they passed what Father said appeared to be a military base, since he recognized some of the types of ships from his earlier travels. The one new thing for both of them, however, was the very fast and VERY loud aircraft that took off and landed at the base. The otters had been exposed only to small and relatively quiet floatplanes up north. These were so loud that they both dived under the water when they saw them approaching.

As they went along, they noticed an increase in boat traffic, even though it was the dead of winter. They took note of any tugs and barges heading back north to see if they had a chance of getting a lift home when the time came. More and more houses appeared along the shore, and both otters sensed they were getting close to their goal.

Then one bright, crisp winter morning, the type that is so special in this part of the world, they rounded a point of land, and laid out before them was a giant harbor with all kinds of vessels. A gleaming city rose up the hills behind the waterfront. Both otters just stopped in the water and tried to take it all in.

Father spotted a small island positioned in the harbor right in front of the city, so they swam to it and went ashore. It looked as if during the summer it would be a bustling marine park but was now completely deserted. They simply sat on the beach and enjoyed the view.

Over the space of several hours, they counted three different ferries plying the waters. One was small and went back and forth from the city to a larger island protecting the mouth of the harbor. The other two ferries, however, were huge. Oscar said they looked to be at least ten times the size of the ferry he was used to near his den. Since these huge ferries all came from the south, Father guessed that they must have come from even larger cities there. Oscar looked back at the city laid out before him and tried to imagine a bigger one, but he just could not.

The two otters decided this would be the base camp for their exploration of the city and harbor and set about making a cozy den.

Chapter eight
City Life

Father and son fashioned a large den with items they found around the park. They made sure they had windows on each side so they could enjoy the view even when they were snug inside. The lights at night were new to them both, and they would spend hours in the evenings just taking them in.

One early morning, they awoke to find that it had snowed during the night, and a soft blanket of white covered everything. The city seemed especially lovely with the white cloth spread across it, and that night, they were treated to a fantastic sight of the lights on the snow. It appeared that the people in the city had put many colored lights on the fronts of their homes and the downtown buildings. They had noticed this earlier, but the snow made them all sparkle in a special way.

Father and Oscar spent their days exploring the entire harbor but always had to be alert due to the activity. They did meet a few animals on their ventures, but they all seemed not as friendly as the ones farther north, barely taking the time to say hello, let alone stopping for an extended meal break. Oscar tried to make friends with a pair of minks he found living under a float on one of the many passageways in the harbor, but they were nothing like his friends back home. They even made fun of him because he was so impressed with their city and said that he was just a country otter. He did not understand the remark, and even Father said he had never heard anything like that from any animal on his many journeys.

They did have one harrowing experience during an outing in the harbor. It was on a clear day with the sun providing a little welcome warmth to their backs as they swam. Moving along a wide side channel, they heard a loud rushing sound and looked around to see what might be making it. Nothing they could see looked like it could be the source of the sound, but it kept getting nearer. Finally, Father turned around and happened to look up, and not a moment too soon. He grabbed Oscar and dove beneath the water just as the pontoons of a floatplane hit the surface right where they had been an instant before.

"Father turned around and happened to look up …"

When they broke the surface again, they could see the plane still taxiing a short distance away. When they made eye contact, there was more than a little relief but also a bit of fear. Oscar had never seen that expression on his father's face before, but he realized that they had both been in real danger and were saved only by Father's quick reaction. Oscar knew if he had been alone without that extra pair of eyes Father had told Daphne about, he might have been killed or severely injured. He gave his father a hug, which was enthusiastically returned.

They both decided that was about as much excitement as they needed for one day and cautiously made their way back to their den on the island. As they shared a meal of freshly gathered shellfish and small fish, they began to talk about heading home. The city had been fun and beautiful and even exciting, but Oscar missed his friends, especially Daphne.

Father even said he wanted to get back and see Mother and the new kits, as well as get together with Omar and Octavia, so they determined they would embark on the northward journey in the morning and curled up for a good night's sleep.

Chapter nine
Homeward Bound

Although the days had started to get longer and the air temperature had risen, the water was still quite cold. Father said they should look around a bit to see if they might find a lift north rather than just setting off swimming. They covered the area just south of their little island and found that, although there were some barges loaded with lumber and some log rafts, everything seemed to be destined for a southerly journey. They returned to the main part of the harbor and finally spotted something that looked promising.

Father had seen a number of barges in his northern travels that were loaded with large shipping containers, automobiles, and even boats or airplanes at times. Here, they saw a smaller barge being loaded with several of the shipping containers, probably destined for one of the logging camps up north. As they swam around the barge, they found, affixed to the side, a ladder, which they could use to climb aboard.

Because Father did not see a tugboat moored near the barge, he said it probably was not quite ready to sail. They found a place under a nearby pier where they could watch the barge until the time was right. It took another couple of days before the last of the containers had been loaded and strapped down. At last, they saw a tugboat approach the dock and lines being attached to the big winches on the boat and to the huge cleats on the barge. As the dock crew was exiting the barge and pulling back the gangplank on the shore side, the two otters clambered up the ladder on the waterside.

Since there was no crew on the barge, Oscar and Father had the entire craft to themselves. The only problem was there was no ready source of food, which concerned Oscar to no end. However, his father explained that when the tug and barge came to narrow passages or had to wait for a tide change, they would have time to go overboard and gather food, which made Oscar feel better.

They soon discovered a narrow gap between two containers which could serve as a temporary den and sat back to enjoy the ride, which they hoped would be much less eventful that their last boat trip. They did watch carefully as the tug and barge left the harbor to make sure they were headed in the right direction and then proceeded to explore the rest of their mobile home.

There was not much of interest on the barge, but they did find some packing blankets that had been left behind and used them to fashion comfortable beds. The barge moved along very slowly, which gave them time to enjoy the scenery from a different perspective than the one they had had coming into the harbor.

Father said they should be on the lookout for the place where they had spent some time with the other otters on the way down so they could stop in for a visit. Oscar thought this was a grand idea since he now had many stories to tell and always loved a chance to relate them. He only hoped that they would not pass the spot at night.

Luckily, on the second day, out they came to the place where they had met the other otters. They slipped over the side and down the ladder and bid a fond farewell to their barge knowing that the rest of the trip home would probably be under their own power.

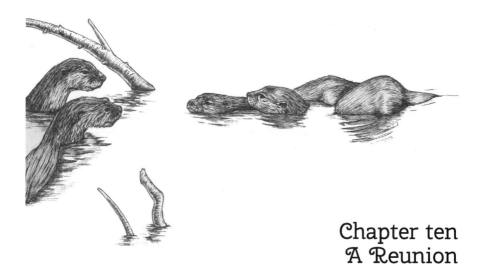

Chapter ten
A Reunion

As the two of them approached the shore, they could see their new friends playing in the shallows, and Oscar remembered that it had been quite some time since he had just enjoyed a playtime with friends. As soon as the other otters recognized the travelers, there was a great commotion with hugs being shared and everyone talking at once.

When the excitement died down, all determined they needed a giant feast. Oscar and Father were more than ready for this and joined in the hunting and gathering with gusto. When they had assembled a huge pile of fish, clams, and oysters on the beach, they all ate until they could not hold another bite. Then it was story time, and they all gathered around to hear tales of the big city. Father deferred to Oscar, who was bursting with enthusiasm.

Oscar regaled the group with the sights and sounds of the city, the beautiful lights and the snow, the hustle and bustle and, of course, their narrow escape from the seaplane. They all seemed to hang on Oscar's every word, but he began to notice a number of the otters appearing to be a bit self-conscious of their more sheltered existence and lack of experience.

All of a sudden, Oscar stopped and told them he had saved the absolute best story till last. Father looked a little surprised since he thought Oscar had told them all. Oscar began by relating his encounter with the minks on the dock in the harbor. He went on to describe their making fun of him and calling him a "country otter." Then he said he had learned the city animals had lost their sense of joy and no longer remembered hospitality, both of which made their "country" lives so full. He ended with a toast to all of his new friends and invited them to enjoy his own hospitality if they ever made the trip north.

It was very quiet for a moment, and then a huge cheer erupted, and all of the otters, including Father, rushed to embrace Oscar. There were more than a few tears of joy, and a firm bond of friendship had been formed. Later, as they were settling in for the night, Father told his son how proud he was of him for making everyone feel at ease.

Father drifted off to sleep thinking about how his young son had matured. He could see in Oscar not only a feeling for the physical well-being of his fellow creatures, as he had in helping to free the wolf from the snare, but also a feeling for the emotional well-being of those around him. He knew this had to come from deep within Oscar, and he had a few regrets in not having been around more to watch his development. He went to sleep with a firm resolve to stop his traveling and spend more time with Mother and all of his offspring.

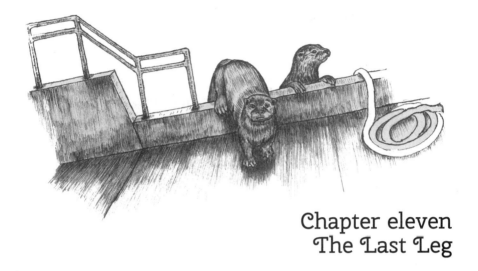

Chapter eleven
The Last Leg

After spending a few days with the other otters, Oscar and his father told them they needed to be moving on home. After one more feast, the two set out on the last leg of their journey. They stopped in at their landlocked ship for a day and found it as they had left it. After paying one last visit to the processing plant for a snack of oysters, they swam north.

As they passed by the rocks where their first boat trip had ended abruptly, they saw that the crab boat was no longer perched atop the rocks. Father said it probably had been salvaged and might be able to be repaired. Both otters joked that if the boat ever set sail again, it would probably not be with the same crew.

They now knew they were getting close to home and swam just a little bit faster. When they sighted the southern tip of Quadra Island, Cape Mudge, they made straight for it instead of making the crossing in the currents at Campbell River. However, by the time they made the point, they were both really tired and spent the night in some driftwood on the beach.

The next morning, they arose early and proceeded up the east side of the island. They saw the little ferry leaving Heriot Bay bound for Cortes, and Oscar mentioned that was about the right size for a ferry. As they passed Mother's den, Father said he was stopping in for a while but he would come up to Oscar's before nightfall. Oscar went on alone and decided he would visit the minks before returning to his den. Little did he know what a good decision that would turn out to be.

He came up on the beach where he and his friends had had so many wonderful parties and went up to the minks' den. He announced himself but was surprised when they did not come right out. Finally, one of the minks poked its head cautiously out the opening but brightened as it recognized Oscar and called to its mate to come out.

They greeted Oscar warmly, but he could see something was bothering them. They told him they had some bad news and then began to relate their most disturbing tale. It seemed that shortly after Oscar and his father had left on their trip a large family of muskrats had come into Hyacinthe Bay. They were a noisy and messy group, and all of the local animals hoped they would swim right on. However, to everyone's dismay, the muskrats discovered Oscar's den and moved in immediately. The minks said the muskrats were terrible neighbors: they made lots of noise, they messed up the beach, and they smelled awful. The muskrats also went around in large groups and were very quarrelsome, bullying the other animals.

Oscar was really upset, especially when thinking how lovely he had made his den and how they must have ruined it. He told the minks his father was going to join him soon and they should get the raccoon brothers and try to come up with a scheme to get rid of the muskrats. One of the minks left to search for the raccoons while the other stayed with Oscar to wait for Father.

Chapter twelve
A Plan Is Hatched

By the time the first mink returned with the raccoon brothers in tow, Father had arrived and been brought up to date on what had happened during their absence. The six of them set to work on a way to get the muskrats out of the den. Both the raccoons and the minks said that, even though the muskrats individually were smaller than the other animals, they always stuck together as a group and were extremely aggressive. The minks and raccoons also pointed out that the entrance to the den was rather narrow and only one of them would be able to get through at a time, making a frontal assault impossible.

One of the group suggested smoking the muskrats out with a fire in front of the opening. The others ruled that idea out, first, by the fact that none of them had any real way of getting fire, second, by what damage the smoke might do to the den, and third, by the possibility that a fire could spread to the surrounding underbrush and cause major destruction.

During the discussion, Oscar had been very quiet and lost in his thoughts. The others just thought he was upset about his home, but at last, he broke his silence and asked the raccoons if they knew where the wolf they had saved from the snare was. The brothers said they had a rough idea of where his lair was, but they were somewhat reluctant to search it out. Oscar offered to go with them and then outlined his plan.

All of the others, including Father, were excited by what Oscar proposed, and the raccoons agreed to go with Oscar to find the wolf. Father and the minks stayed behind to make some preparations on the beach behind Oscar's den.

It took Oscar and the raccoons quite a while to locate the wolf's lair in the deep forest, but when they did, he welcomed them and thanked them once more for saving his life. Oscar and the brothers explained the situation at Oscar's den and the plan they had to get rid of the muskrats. The wolf was happy to oblige, not only because of the debt he felt to the three of them but also, as he explained, he had had a few encounters with muskrats and found them to be a most disagreeable lot.

They made their way back to the little beach on the islet where Father and the minks were waiting, but did not get there until well after dark. They could hear the rowdy noises of the invaders across the still water, which only served to make their task even more important.

Oscar went with Father to the entrance to the secret passage in the back of his den and was pleased to see that Father and the minks had cleaned it up and made room for an easy access for both Oscar and his father. Father said he had gone all the way up to the place where the tunnel entered the den and found the wall still intact, meaning the muskrats had not discovered the secret passage.

When Oscar and Father returned to the rest of the group, Oscar detailed what each needed to do. They decided they should make their move at first light in the morning after a good night's rest, but they were all too excited to get any sleep. Instead, they rehearsed what they were to do till they had it all memorized.

The noise from the den finally died down, indicating the muskrats were asleep, which suited the attackers perfectly. As soon as the sky turned to a light gray, the seven comrades made their way silently across the channel and took up their positions.

Oscar, Father, and the wolf went straight to the opening to the secret passage, while the raccoons and minks took up positions on each side of the front entrance. The two otters entered the passage and moved up toward the den and made sure they each had a firm footing. Then Oscar gave the signal to the wolf.

Chapter thirteen
The Attack at Dawn

At Oscar's signal, the wolf gave out a low rumbling growl, which gradually increased in intensity. At first, nothing happened; all was still inside the den. The wolf began again, and the otters could hear stirrings among the muskrats and some concerned discussion. By the end of the third growl, the wolf was at full throat, and all the muskrats were awake.

On the second signal from Oscar, the wolf put back his head and let forth his very best howl. At that moment, Oscar and Father broke through the back wall of the den and made as much noise as they possibly could, cuffing some of the muskrats as they did so. It was far too dark for any of the muskrats to see what was coming in the back door, but there was no mistaking the sound of a wolf's howl.

"They turned to see a determined band of two otters, two raccoons, two minks, and coming around the beach, one very large and very fierce wolf."

As the howl came again, the entire pack of muskrats made for the front door, jamming into each other as they attempted their frantic exit. As they came through the opening, the raccoons and minks were ready to run their sharp claws across their flanks as they hustled toward the water. Not one of them escaped without many scratches, and when they were finally in the water a safe distance away from whatever so rudely had awakened them, they turned to see a determined band of two otters, two raccoons, two minks, and coming around the beach, one very large and very fierce wolf.

The wolf glared at them with his fearsome yellow eyes and gave one more howl, just for effect. At that, the muskrats turned as one and swam out of the bay, around the islet, and were never seen again in the area.

The seven were elated, and they congratulated each other on a successful campaign. Oscar personally thanked each of his friends and gave them a big hug, except for the wolf, whose paw he shook.

The smaller animals offered to help Oscar clean up the mess made by the muskrats. Of course, the wolf could be of little help there so he excused himself saying he probably should get out of the area and back to his lair since he might have awakened some humans and they might come looking for him with guns.

When the six went back into the den, they were dismayed at what they saw. It looked as if something had come in and stirred up the interior leaving it in total shambles. Also, the thick smell of the muskrats was almost too much for their nostrils. They set about straightening the place up, and after a few hours, they had hauled out all of the trash and had the area livable again. The smell was another matter, however.

They left the back door open so the air could pass through and then gathered pine boughs to try to cover the scent. They thought it would eventually do the trick, but Oscar was going to have to find temporary lodgings. Father was sure that either Omar or Octavia would be happy to put up their brother for a little while, and that seemed to settle everything.

There was one other thing on Oscar's mind that he needed to take care of so he thanked his father and friends one more time and told them he would be back in a week or so and headed to the east.

Epilogue

The spring morning was as lovely as any you could possibly imagine. The sun glistened off the crystalline water, and a soft breeze whispered through the boughs of the small evergreens. In a cozy den, a mother river otter was giving birth to a pair of offspring. Daphne lay admiring her beautiful twins, and her thoughts turned to Oscar. As if her thoughts had been some sort of magical magnet, she looked up to see him in the entrance to her den.

With tears of joy running down her face, she rose and embraced him. They did not speak; they did not have to. Oscar looked down at the two little ones and tears welled up in him, too. Oscar and Daphne curled up around the newborns, and they knew all was right in their world.

As all odysseys must end with the return home of the wayfarer, so does this one. However, as we all know, the end of one journey is simply the beginning of the next.

About the Author

Bruce Bradburn lives with his wife, Meg Holgate, an accomplished artist, in Seattle, Washington. Born in Chicago, he has lived in Seattle since 1947. He graduated from Lakeside School in 1959 and from Northwestern University in 1964, with a degree in industrial engineering.

His three children and nine grandchildren all live in Seattle and are frequent visitors to the Inn at Bradburn Landing in British Columbia, where this book is set. He enjoys cooking in the magnificent kitchen described in the story, as do all of the children who love to share the experience.

Hopefully, the stories about this beautiful area of the world will inspire all who read them to take an active interest in preserving the resources and wildlife of the region for enjoyment by many future generations.

Coming soon!
More tales from Quadra Island...

LUNAR LARCENY

by
Bruce Bradburn
Illustrations by Rhys Haug

CHAPTER ONE

"Good morning, Chicagoland. It's going to be another scorcher, and don't expect any relief from the humidity. I hope your A/C is in working order."

Will roused from his slumber to the grating sound of the early-morning disc jockey, the sun blazing in his window, and a disgusted reminder that he had forgotten to turn off his alarm. Yesterday was the last day of school for the summer, and he certainly did not have to get up at his usual time. He tried to ignore the obvious and pulled the covers up over his head, but the sun was just too bright, and the DJ just would not shut up.

"It's 8:07, and volumes are already building on all major roadways. On the Dan Ryan and Kennedy, we are looking at bumper-to-bumper. Why are you all out there? Don't you know it's summer? Why don't you go on vacation? Get out of town for heaven's sake; let the tourists deal with this mess."

Will finally summoned enough energy to roll over, hit the snooze button, and pull the covers back over his head. At least the DJ was gone, but the sun was still beating on him with the intensity of a laser.

He fought back as hard as he could and was just about able to get back to sleep when . . .

"Well now you've done it! You two yokels on the Kennedy who HAD to go and touch bumpers and not make it to the shoulder have now made about ten thousand people late for work! I told you you should be on vacation. When are you EVER going to listen to me???"

Will growled and groped for the clock radio, this time making sure he hit the Off button and not the Snooze. However, it was too late; now he was fully awake.

He stuffed arms into his robe and started to make his way to the kitchen for a bowl of cereal. He did take a moment to look out of his window as he did nearly every morning, marveling at the sight of Lake Michigan as far as he could see, and he was not even looking the length of the lake, but across it to the east. The nice part of living on the for-tieth floor of a lakefront high-rise was the unobstructed view. He was stirred from his reverie by a growl from his stomach, which was even louder than the one from his mouth when the DJ had blasted back in with the traffic report.

Will shuffled into the kitchen and found his parents, Doug and Judy, having coffee and toast at the table. They both looked up and smiled at their son.

"Good morning," said Mom. "You're up early for your first day of your summer vacation."

"I forgot to turn off my alarm. School ending on a Wednesday threw me off track. I always remember to turn it off on the weekends."

"Well, I'm glad you're up and about," said Dad. "Grab yourself a bowl of cereal and join us. I have some really interesting news for you."

Will stopped in his tracks. The last time his parents had had "some interesting news" for him, they had enrolled him in piano lessons that caused him to miss every single Saturday Bulls game. Only after he had demonstrated a decided lack of musical talent and even less of an inclination to practice did his parents release him from the lessons, and it was well after the basketball season had ended.

Will did manage to get a bowl and the cereal from the cupboard and the containers of milk and juice from the fridge and drag himself to the table with all of the enthusiasm of someone about to consume his last meal.

"OK," he finally was able to mutter after sitting down, "what is this really great news?"

"Something has come up at the office. We are going to be moving into a larger space, so about half of us are going to take off for a month and let the business run with a skeleton crew while the construction people and movers do their thing."

"So, if you're not going into the office, just what are you going to be doing for a month?" Will asked.

"That's where the really interesting news comes in," said his dad. "You do remember your Uncle Bob and Aunt Angie, don't you?"

"Yeah. They're the ones who live way out, like in the Oregon Territory, right?"

"Well, it's Seattle, Washington, actually, and they have a son, Michael, who is your age, remember?"

"OK, so where are we going with this?"

"We're going out west," interjected Judy, happily. "Isn't that great?"

"What's in Seattle? They don't even have an NBA franchise."

"They did have one," responded his father.

"Oh right! They lost it to Oklahoma City. How lame is that!"

"Well," said Dad, "it isn't basketball season, and we won't be spending much time in Seattle, anyway, which gets me to the best part of the news."

"Oh, you mean it gets better?"

"Lots! It seems that your Uncle Bob and Aunt Angie have bought a place up in British Columbia, and they have invited us to join them and Michael for an entire month on Quadra Island. Isn't that grand?"

"What's so grand about being stuck on an island in the frozen north for a whole month with that nerdy Michael?"

Judy could see that this was not going as well as she and Doug had hoped when the idea had come up, so she tried to lighten things up a bit.

"This place that Bob and Angie have is right on the water, and they have a boat and kayaks, and there are deer and raccoons and eagles, and the water's warm, and there are clams and oysters, and there are great hikes and places to bicycle and explore, and you will have someone your own age to share the adventures with," Judy rattled off so quickly that Will could not work in objections.

"If you mean Michael," said Will, "I kinda doubt that. I remember him as a geeky bookworm with horn-rimmed glasses who didn't know a free throw from a lay-up and was a real runt."

Judy could see that Doug was starting to get irritated, so she tried a different tack.

"You obviously haven't looked at their Christmas cards in the last few years. Michael is still an A-student, but he has grown up to be about your size, and he doesn't wear glasses at all any more. He has also turned into quite a competitive swimmer, and he rows crew."

She got up from the table and went to her desk in a corner of the kitchen and rummaged through a drawer.

"Ah," she said, "Here is the picture that was with this year's card. Take a look."

Will accepted the photograph and held it out as if it were dusted with anthrax. To his great surprise, the young man standing with his aunt and uncle bore no relationship to the picture in his mind of his cousin. This Michael was as tall as he was and appeared to be in excellent physical shape. Will returned the photograph to his mother and thought for a minute. He still was not sure if he wanted to spend a whole month on an island in the far north with a bunch of wild animals, but at least the company might not be as bad as he had originally thought.

"So, when is this expedition supposed to take place?" Will asked his parents.

"We had planned to leave here in about a week," said Dad, sensing a slight change in his son's attitude. "We thought we would stay a couple of days in Seattle before heading up to Quadra Island. Uncle Bob has managed to get tickets for us to go to a Mariners game, and I thought you might like to see them take on the Yankees. The last leg of the journey to Quadra is via floatplane, which will be a new experience for all of us."

All of a sudden, this did not sound like a death sentence to Will, and he began firing questions at his parents at such a rate that they could not keep up. Judy went over to her desk again and fired up her computer.

"Come over here, Will. Uncle Bob and Aunt Angie e-mailed me some pictures of their place in Canada. I think you'll find them interesting."

There were about a dozen pictures. Will saw no frozen tundra, only a stunningly beautiful setting. The water was crystal clear, and the rocks and trees were like none he had ever seen. Uncle Bob and Aunt Angie's house was marvelous, and the very last picture was of what appeared to be an old-fashioned caboose.

"Do they actually have a railroad on this island?" Will asked his parents.

"No," responded his father, "Uncle Bob had that built, and it's where you and Michael will sleep. It has a full bathroom, a bunkroom, a living room with a woodstove, and a TV with a DVD player. Uncle Bob has a huge collection of movies, and they also have a new Xbox."

This not only no longer sounded like a death sentence but also was starting to sound like a fun time..

"Well, I guess it looks as if you have already made the plans, so I might as well come along."

Will tried to make it sound as if he were resigned to go, but he was unable to conceal his excitement.

"I think I'll go to my room and look over what I might want to take," said Will, getting up from the table.

Uncharacteristically, he put his dishes in the sink and returned the milk and juice containers to the fridge and the cereal box to the cupboard.

Will had no sooner left the room than his parents winked at each other and did a quiet high-five across the breakfast table.